Daniel's Desire

CALLIE HUTTON

ISBN-10: 1543088163
ISBN-13: 978-1543088168

ABOUT THE BOOK

When Confederate soldier, Lt. Daniel McCoy makes his escape from a Union prison toward the end of the Civil War, his only thought is to get as far away from enemy territory as possible. But he doesn't count on saving young widow Rosemarie Wilson's life from an infected leg wound.

Rosemarie has no use for Rebels soldiers, having lost everything, including her husband, the last time they came to her home. However, Daniel has not only saved her life, but is sticking around to help with the farm and her three children until she recovers.

With Union soldiers searching for him, every day Daniel remains puts him in danger. Or is the beautiful widow who has captured his heart the greater risk?.

DEDICATION

To my niece, Rosemarie, whose name I borrowed for this story.

NOTE FROM THE AUTHOR

Oliver P. Morton was the governor of Indiana at the close of the Civil War, and had been a circuit judge before becoming governor. The blurb in the newspaper Rosemarie read, attributed to Governor Morton about his feelings on the war, were his actual words.

The 'speech' he gave later on in his parlor to Rosemarie, were my words, but what I imagined the man would have said.

During the Civil War, the citizens of Indianapolis did, indeed, provide food, clothing, and nursing services for the Confederate soldiers kept there. The Union prison camps held back supplies for their prisoners because the inmates being detained in the Confederate prisons were not offered much in the way of necessities. That was due to the fact that near the end of the war, the Confederacy could barely feed their own soldiers. When an exchange of prisoners was suggested, President Lincoln refused, hoping that would help end the war.

CHAPTER ONE

March, 1865
Camp Morton, Indianapolis

Not a sliver of moonlight, no campfires burning. Darkness covered Confederate soldier, Lieutenant Daniel McCoy, like a shroud. His heart pounded, blocking any sound to warn him of danger, of rapid footsteps in pursuit, or the click of metal before a bullet entered his body. A befitting end for a prison escapee.

He stood like a statue to calm his racing heart and allow his eyes time to adjust. Not that it had been bright in the dingy hellhole he'd just left. The one where he'd spent the last month digging his way to freedom. A place where smallpox, cholera, and dysentery ran rampant, and men died screaming, or crying the name of a wife or sweetheart.

Deep voices carried over the night air from where two guards met. One sentry struck a flint to light his cigar, revealing their dirty war-battled faces, as they spoke in low tones. As always, the twang of their accent grated on his nerves. He moved deeper into the shadows until the soldiers separated, each going a different direction.

He took a deep breath and eyed the stables.

Too risky to steal a horse.

After the enemies' footsteps died away, Daniel's long strides covered the open area to the safety of the trees. Lack of exercise over the past months had taken a toll on his body, and his lungs burned from the short sprint. He eased behind a large oak, watching, waiting for an alarm to sound.

Silence.

His index finger and thumb rubbed the cool metal of the heavy ring tucked in his pocket. He'd stolen it back from the drunken Union soldier while he'd slept. Once again, the heirloom rested where it belonged. With him—a McCoy.

Sweat beaded his forehead, and he took gulps of the damp night air before bending to empty his stomach of the last putrid meal they'd fed him. Truth be told, if it hadn't been for the local citizens of Indianapolis, the Confederates would probably all be dead. The residents showed immense compassion toward the prisoners, providing the necessary food, clothing, and nursing to keep most of the inmates alive.

The guards made another pass, and still no shouts came from within the prison walls. Despite the cold, Lieutenant McCoy wiped sweat from his forehead, then picked his way through the forest surrounding the Union camp. The sound of his panting echoed off the trees as he picked up the pace and stumbled over small roots and animal holes in the dark. He raced to the bank of the White River, waded into the mud and silt, and dove into the icy water. The shock of the cold took his breath away, but with strong strokes, he swam from the cursed prison.

After nine long months in hell, he breathed free air.

Johnson County, Indiana

"Mama, can I get you some tea?"

Rosemarie Wilson eased heavy eyelids open and

attempted to smile with dry, cracked lips at her eight-year-old son, Chandler. The frown on his pale face tore at her heart.

"No thank you. Just look after your sister and brother." She shifted on the bed, struggling to relieve the throbbing pain in her leg. Black dots danced before her eyes at the movement, and her stiff fingers grabbed the worn patchwork quilt to control the dizziness and nausea. She raised her head from the pillow and moved the blanket from her leg. The smell from the festering cut on her right calf, where the axe had sliced almost to the bone, scared her. She'd cleaned it after the accident as best she could. However, the awkward position of the wound made the stitches she put in jerky and uneven.

Tears slid down her cheeks as life ebbed from her weary body. She'd used so much of her strength trying to keep the farm going after a band of Confederate soldiers had swooped in a few months ago and taken just about everything they'd owned. Shortly after, she'd laid her husband of nine years to rest in the little plot under the elm tree behind the house. Dead from a bullet wound after one of the soldiers had shot him.

Damn this war, and everything it's taken from my family!

Another tear slipped from her eye and landed on the thin nightgown covering her shoulder. Chandler's voice drifted in through the bedroom door, as he spoke to his younger brother and sister in the kitchen. Five-year-old Amelia balked at having leftover oatmeal for lunch. Several more tears joined the first one, and Rosemarie's heart throbbed so hard it hurt. She closed her eyes against the pain and drifted into the welcoming oblivion of sleep.

Rays from bright sunshine seeped beneath the wooden shutters on the bedroom window, bathing her face in light, forcing her to turn aside. Her body burned with heat.

If I could just have a drink of water.

She listened for a minute, terrified at the silence that greeted her. Where were her children? "Chandler?" Her voice rasped.

No answer. She raised herself up on one elbow and called louder. Still no answer. Tears of pain and frustration gathered in her eyes.

Dear God, please help me.

Did God even listen to her anymore? She'd prayed all her life, always had faith. Even when her father had sold her into marriage not much older than a child, she knelt and prayed for Hans to be a good man. Cold and stern, and not the man she would have chosen for herself, her husband had nevertheless provided well for her and their children. The three beautiful children the good Lord had blessed her with.

Now the only parent they had left lay dying.

□□

Daniel spied the small farmhouse from half a mile away. The sun setting behind the clapboard structure bathed it in an ethereal glow. Three children sat on the front porch, huddled together in the cold. The biggest one rose and stared in his direction. Then the child hurried into the house, leaving the two smaller ones outside.

As Daniel moved closer, he expected an adult to appear at the front door, and braced himself to run. All he wanted from the farmer was a drink from his well, and he'd be on his way. After walking the entire day, he hadn't passed even one creek to ease his thirst.

The two smaller children turned toward the door as if someone spoke to them. They immediately got up, and holding hands, entered the house. Still no adult ventured out. Did someone stand at the window, ready to shoot? Indeed, in this part of the country he was the enemy, but his dirty and worn Confederate uniform wouldn't be recognized from a distance, so he pressed on.

Unconsciously, his hand drifted to his pocket to rub the ring. He needed to move further south before the

Union soldiers found him. One escaped Rebel would be inconsequential, but since he'd been designated one of the camp medics after a Union doctor had been sent to the fields, they would come after him. He'd hated abandoning his fellow Confederates, but very few would survive, and there wasn't much he could have done for them.

Except pray for their souls as they died.

Fatigue washed over him as he approached the porch. If the owner approved, Daniel would quench his thirst, then crawl into the farmer's barn and sleep for the night. Maybe even get a bucket of water to wash his body. His clothes were still stiff from the mud in the river.

A window over the front porch was open, a white lace curtain blowing in the breeze. The moment he set his foot on the bottom step, the distinct sound of a gun being readied caught his attention. Within seconds, a young boy stepped out the door, the business end of the shotgun pointed straight at Daniel's chest.

"Git off my property." The child's pale face resembled new snow. His ragged pants had been patched, but not washed in a while. Lines normally found on an adult's face bracketed either side of his young mouth.

Daniel raised both hands, palms facing the boy. "Son, I only want to get a drink of water from your well. Can you ask your pa to step out?"

"Git off, I said." The shotgun wavered, and the boy's eyes narrowed.

Daniel backed away, keeping his hands in the air. He didn't want the kid to accidently shoot him out of fear. "Can you tell me how far to the next town, then?"

"You a Reb?" The boy's voice trembled.

"Yes, but I'm not here to hurt you or your family. I just want some water, and I'll be on my way." He slowly lowered his hands, but kept them in front of him, palms out. "Is your pa home?"

Tears sprung to the child's eyes as he shook his head.

"Your ma?"

5

"Why do you wanna know?"

Daniel sighed. "I would like permission for a drink of water from your well, and maybe to sleep in your barn for the night."

The two smaller children he'd spotted earlier came out the door, and stood behind the older boy. The little girl, with long brown curls cascading down her back, took her fingers out of her tiny rosebud mouth and spoke. "Our ma is bad sick. Chan thinks she's gonna die."

"Quiet down, Amelia, and go back into the house. And take Jace with you." The boy who Daniel assumed was Chan jerked his head in the direction of the door, his face flushed.

Amelia focused her huge blue eyes on Daniel. "Can you help our ma, mister?"

"Amelia!" Chan lowered the gun, and faced his sister. "I said git back into the house."

"Son, look at me." Daniel spoke in a low voice, and didn't move from his spot. The boy continued to grip the gun, but no longer pointed the thing at him.

"What?" He wiped tears on his sleeve, then raised the gun back up.

"Where's your pa?"

Amelia spoke up again, moving to the edge of the porch. "Our pa is behind the house."

He blew out a sigh of relief. "Can you fetch him for me?"

"Can't." She shook her head and stuck her fingers back into her mouth. The younger boy, not much more than a baby, came to the edge of the porch and started down the steps.

"Jace, git back here!" Chan lowered the gun again and grabbed for his brother.

Daniel directed his comments to Amelia. "Can I go around to the back of the house and speak with your pa?"

She shook her curly head again.

"Why not?"

6

"Pa died," Jace lisped in a baby voice, big blue eyes riveted on him.

Daniel's shoulders slumped, and he looked at Chan. "Is your pa dead?"

The boy gave a quick nod, and raised the gun again. "Now git off my property. We don't want no Rebs around here. You already done took everything we had."

The young piercing eyes reminded him he stood in enemy territory. With the pa dead, and the ma so sick she didn't come out to investigate, these children were in a lot of trouble. The oldest boy still regarded him with narrowed eyes, even though the younger boy and little girl had advanced down the steps and now stood right in front of him, watching him with huge eyes.

"Can you fix my ma, mister?" Amelia asked as she reached for her little brother's hand.

Daniel's heart seized at the serious situation. He needed to look at their mother, but it didn't appear Chan would let him. No doubt he had reason to mistrust Confederates.

"Chan. Is that your name?" He spoke softly to the boy who continued to swipe at his eyes. The kid seemed about to fall apart, but with a shaky arm still managed to point the gun in his direction.

The boy ignored the question, however Daniel continued. "My name is Daniel McCoy, and I know a little bit about healing. Can I at least look at your ma?"

"No Reb is gonna touch my ma."

"Chandler, I want Mama to get better." Amelia burst into tears and wrapped her tiny arms around Daniel's leg, leaning against him as if he were a pillar of strength. Something these children sorely needed.

What a dilemma. One look at his sister, and the little boy also began to wail, and grabbed his other leg.

"Chandler, please." Daniel patted the two children on their heads, as he appealed to the boy. "Let me say hello to your ma. I won't touch her, or do anything to upset her."

The boy hesitated, so he added, "You can keep your gun pointed at me the whole time."

Apparently those were the magic words because the boy lowered the gun and wiped his eyes once more. "All right. But I'll be watchin' you."

The minute Daniel stepped into the small living room, his nostrils twitched with the smell of disease.

Dear God, what's wrong with the woman?

"Where's your ma?"

Daniel followed Chandler down a short dark hallway. The boy gestured to the open door with his head. Daniel stepped in and his breathing hitched.

A woman lay on a large bed, dark circles under her closed eyes. He would have pronounced her already dead if not for the very slight movement of her chest and the deep flush of fever on her skin. He moved to the bed, and grasped her wrist. Her eyes remained closed, her pulse weak, but steady.

He turned toward Chandler, who now held the gun at his side, his sister and brother huddled against him. "Can I remove the sheet to look at where she's hurt?"

His eyes never leaving his mother, the boy gave one curt nod.

Daniel lifted the sheet and almost lost the little bit of the meal he'd had a few hours ago. The woman had an infected gash on her leg. The wound had been partially stitched and bloody pus oozed from it, dripping onto the stained sheet below. He laid the back of his hand against her forehead. She burned with fever.

Maybe he wouldn't be able to save her leg, but he had to try. He could cauterize it, but since the injury showed no sign of gangrene, it would be best if he cleaned the wound and re-stitched it. Suturing would be easier on the woman than searing her skin.

"Can you fix her?" Amelia's small voice ripped into his gut.

Truth, or false assurances? God, they were all so young.

Daniel walked to where the children stood in the doorway and got down on one knee. "I can try, Amelia, and I will work very hard. But you must do something for me." He looked at Chandler and Jace. "All of you. You must pray. The best prayers you ever said."

Three small heads bobbed. Apparently, the children were no strangers to prayer.

He rose. "Chandler, where does your ma keep her medical things?"

The child laid the gun on a table, led him to the mudroom, and pointed to a shelf. "She keeps everything up there."

"Thanks. I want you to heat some water on the stove for me. Do you have a fire going?"

The boy squared his shoulders. "I can start one."

"Good. Next I want you to find me a pair of scissors and an old sheet, or some kind of clean rags I can rip up for a bandage."

"What can I do?" Amelia leaned her head back, almost falling over backward to meet his eyes.

"You can help us get things ready. Then, I'll need you to be very, very brave and take your little brother to the parlor and wait there with him while I see to your mama's leg. Can you do that?"

"Will Chandler be with you?"

"Yes. I need his help, but it's important for you and your little brother to stay in the parlor."

Her tiny chin quivered, and he knelt in front of her again. "I know you want to stay with your mama, but you need to be a brave, big girl and take care of Jace."

She wiped tears from her eyes, but whispered, "Okay."

Even having Chandler in the room would be difficult with the work Daniel had to do, but he needed a second pair of hands, no matter how young.

"Chandler, what happened to your mama's leg?"

Daniel entered the kitchen, his hands filled with herbs, medicines and salves from the woman's medical supplies.

"She was chopping wood and the axe slipped and cut her leg."

Daniel winced at the pain the poor woman must have endured. "How long ago?"

"Day before yesterday."

A mild sense of relief swept through him. At least she wasn't so far gone there wouldn't be any chance of saving her, and the leg.

"I'll have to use a needle and some thread to sew up your mama's cut. Where are her sewing things?"

"I know." Amelia had followed him into the kitchen, and with a big smile at being able to help, she pointed to a shelf in the kitchen to the left of the stove. "Mama keeps her needles and stuff up there."

"Thank you, little lady."

She blushed and ducked her head. Her fingers slid into her mouth.

"What's your mama's name?" Although the woman would be far better off if she didn't awaken, he'd like to use her name if she did. Cutting away the ineffective stitches and dead skin, cleaning a festering wound, and then sewing it up was enough to fell a large man. What would the procedure do to the delicate woman in the next room? He stiffened his spine. If he didn't do it she would lose her leg, and most likely her life.

Amelia removed her fingers from her mouth and furrowed her brows in such a way Daniel almost chuckled. "Mama's name is Mama."

Chandler entered the room. "Her real name is Rosemarie. Rosemarie Wilson." He held up a worn petticoat. "Mama's skirt is all I could find to make bandages."

"That's fine, son. See if you can tear it into strips for me."

Daniel poured a portion of the heated water into a

large bowl next to the sink. He scooped out soft soap from the container next to the water pump, and using the bowl of hot water and soap, scrubbed his hands, then rinsed them with cool water from the pump.

He turned, shaking his wet hands. Three young faces all stared at him, wide-eyed and terrified.

Dear God. She's their only parent.

Taking a deep breath, he smiled at Amelia. "Go with your little brother into the parlor. You can start saying your prayers now."

She ran to Daniel, wrapping her thin arms around his thigh. "I'm scared. I don't want Mama to die." Then she burst into tears.

He reached down and lifted her in his arms. "Remember when we talked about you being really brave for your brother?"

She nodded, and wiped the tears from her cheeks with the heels of her hands.

"Now is when you have to do that. All right?"

Amelia bit her lower lip and ducked her head. He set her back on her feet and nudged her toward the parlor. "Take Jace in there. We'll call you when we're done, and you can come see your mama."

The little girl wrapped her arm around her baby brother and moved him forward. "Come on, Jace. We'll say prayers like Mama taught us."

Daniel returned to the sink and again washed his hands. Then picking up the supplies, he handed a few to a very pale Chandler. "Let's go."

CHAPTER TWO

Daniel ran his sleeve over his forehead, lowered his aching body to the front porch step, and leaned his tired head on the railing. He took in large gulps of fresh air, breathing in the scent of Indiana dirt in winter. A fresh and clean odor, mixed with the scent of manure and hay.

Two hours of bending over Mrs. Wilson's bed, watching her writhe in agony as he worked, had just about done him in. Twice, Chandler left the room to empty his stomach, and only the hell Daniel had endured at Camp Morton kept him from doing the same.

Mercifully, the woman passed out as he put in the first stitch. If only he'd had some chloroform, he could have spared her the torture of cutting away the dead skin and dousing the cut with whiskey. She'd refused the liquor he'd wanted her to drink, but snapped in two a piece of wood he'd given her to hold between her teeth. Rosemarie Wilson was one damn strong woman.

Goose bumps rose on his skin as cold air blew against his sweat-soaked shirt. He shivered, but kept his place on the porch. The fresh air wafting over him took away some of the sour smell still in his nostrils.

He inhaled deeply, the Indiana air a sharp contrast to

the sultry breezes of Virginia. Eventually, the cold sent him back into the scant warmth of the house.

Amelia and Jace lay curled together on the cold floor, like a couple of kittens. Chandler chose to stay with his mama, but even before Daniel had left the room, the boy's soft snores brought a smile to his lips. Daniel placed his hands on his hips and regarded the two younger Wilson children. They would freeze before morning.

Wandering around a stranger's house felt a bit odd. He found the children's bedroom, with one bed and a small cot pushed against opposite walls. Apparently the boys shared the bed, and Amelia slept in the cot. He returned to the parlor, and lifted the little girl. She opened one sleepy eye and yawned, then stuck her fingers into her mouth. Her soft, warm body rolled toward him and she rubbed her face against his shirt. He placed her in the cot and removed her shoes, then drew up the plaid quilt over the little body now coiled into a ball. Then he returned to the parlor and did the same for Jace.

As tired as he was, he had to see to Mrs. Wilson. Her dry skin had burned with fever when he'd left her a short while ago. Returning to the kitchen, he splashed cool water into a pan, grabbed the last of the torn petticoat, and entered the bedroom. Chandler had fallen over, his thin body, all spindly arms and legs, splayed over the chair. Daniel gathered him in his arms, and carried him across the hall, then placed him in the bed with Jace before returning to Rosemarie's bedroom.

Moonlight cast the room in silver shadows. The woman slept in a deep, fever-induced slumber. Every once in a while she would moan, her brow furrowed. He drew the sheet down, exposing the pale skin above her chemise and below her drawers. With her leg now wrapped in clean cloths, no evidence of fresh blood or pus stained the makeshift bandage. Tomorrow, he would remove the dirty sheet she lay on and replace it with a fresh one.

Tomorrow?

No. He'd done his duty. When the sun rose, he would instruct Chandler on how to take care of his mama and be on his way. Daniel took a big risk sticking around.

As he bathed her soft skin with the cool water, he considered this woman's predicament. Alone with three children, with no one to help her work the farm, how would she keep them all from starving? His gut clenched, but he shoved the picture from his mind. The family would be fine. A lot of women in both the North and South were keeping home and hearth together while their menfolk fought.

How many of them are laid up with a seriously injured leg?

"Hans?" The raspy whisper jarred him from his thoughts.

"No."

A lone tear leaked from her eye and slid down her flushed cheek. "Leg hurts." She thrashed on the bed, tossing her head back and forth. "So hot."

Daniel reached for the glass of cold water on the small table next to the bed, and raising her head, held the liquid to her parched lips. "Drink."

She took a few sips, then turned her head away. He settled her back on the pillow, and her eyes opened. Glazed with fever and pain, she regarded him. "Who are you?"

"A friend."

Her body tensed and her eyes widened. "My children?"

"Sound asleep in their beds. You need to rest."

Her gaze roamed from his face to his dirty, torn uniform. "You a Reb?" Her lips curled as she spit out the words.

"Yes, but I'm not going to hurt you or your family. I want to help."

Two more tears tracked down her cheeks, then she closed her eyes and returned to a deep sleep as he continued to wipe her down with the cool water.

Daniel waved his hand in front of his face to chase away the insect tickling him. As it returned, he waved once more. This insect must have been huge because it began to shake his shoulder.

"Mister, why are you sleeping in my ma's bed?"

His eyes popped open and met the gaze of two pale blue eyes surrounded by thick black lashes. He sat up, and ran his hand down his face. Amelia stood in front of him, holding Jace's hand. And Daniel was, indeed, in Rosemarie Wilson's bed.

The pan with the water he'd been cooling her with sat on the floor. He must have set it there before he fell asleep, but had no memory of it. Never in his life had he been so tired he didn't remember his movements.

"Good morning, Miss Amelia," he said.

"Is my ma all better now?" With the trust of a child, she climbed onto the bed and settled on his lap. Jace imitated his sister, and sat alongside him.

"Not yet, but I think maybe later today she'll start to feel a bit better."

"How's ma?" Chandler stood in the open doorway, rubbing his eyes.

"She's sleeping right now." He laid his palm on her forehead. "Her fever seems a little lower, and that's good."

Jace pulled on his shirt sleeve. "I'm hungwy."

Three sets of blue eyes gazed at him, who was the only adult in the room not unconscious. "Well, let's go into the kitchen and have some breakfast."

"I can fix breakfast." Chandler's eyes narrowed. The boy had recovered his distrust of the stranger in his ma's room.

"No, Chandler." Amelia turned to Daniel. "All he cooks is oatmeal. I hate oatmeal."

His experience with children pretty much non-existent, Daniel drew on childhood battles with his brother, Stephen, to attempt a compromise. "Maybe

Chandler can make oatmeal, and we'll find something to go with it." He stood and lifted Jace off the bed. "I think we should leave your ma to rest."

Amelia placed her small hand in his large one as they walked to the kitchen. Her hand felt so light and delicate, it tickled his palm. Two weeks ago he'd used these large hands to dig his way out of prison, and today he played nursemaid to three children.

He hadn't paid much attention to the house last night. In addition to the darkness, his concern for the woman blocked everything else from his mind. Now as he looked around the kitchen, his stomach dropped. After only a few days with their mama laid up, the place was a mess.

Dirty dishes tilted dangerously alongside the sink where he'd placed them when he pumped water. More dishes sat on the table, with crusting oatmeal in the bottom and sides of the bowls. Milk had splashed and dried on the floor, and a river of molasses flowed across the table.

"I tried to clean up, but Amelia and Jace kept crying and trying to get to Ma." Chandler's face flushed, his stance belligerent.

"It's all right, son. If we all work together, the kitchen will be clean in no time, then we'll have breakfast."

"But not oatmeal." Amelia stuck her fingers in her mouth and shook her head.

Daniel brought in the last of the wood from the box behind the house. He started a fire in the stove to provide warmth to the small house.

With all of them contributing—although Jace caused more problems than help—they got the room in order. Daniel found a few eggs in a bowl on the near-empty pantry shelf, scrambled them up and added that to the breakfast of oatmeal. Then he sliced the last of a loaf of bread and slapped a jar of honey alongside it.

So much for his plans to leave at first light. Food

supplies were low, the woman in the next room could still die, and three children all sat, looking at him expectantly. He pinched the bridge of his nose with, as his other hand slipped into his pocket where he fingered the ring, its inner rim etched with the words *Honorem et Officium*— Honor and Duty. The motto of the McCoy family, drilled into his head since childhood.

The ring had been in his family for generations. Passed from father to son, Daniel had received it from his papa on his deathbed. Honor in his dealings with others, and duty to those in need. And the Wilsons were definitely in need.

"Chandler, can you and Amelia clean up from breakfast while I look around? I'd like to see what food supplies your mama has."

"Everything's gone," Amelia piped up. "Damn Rebels took 'em all."

Daniel bit the inside of his cheek to keep from bursting out with laughter. Apparently the little girl mimicked her mama.

"Ma said no cussin', Amelia." Chandler poked his sister in the arm.

"Ouch." Her eyes filled with tears and her chin trembled as she rubbed her arm.

Time for a diversion.

Daniel clapped his hands. "Amelia, instead of helping Chandler, I'm going to give you a job to help your mama."

"You will?" Her eyes grew big as she climbed from her chair.

"Yes. Come with me."

"Me, too." Jace joined his sister as they walked the short hallway, then entered Mrs. Wilson's bedroom.

Daniel retrieved the pan from the floor, then returned to the kitchen to fill it with water.

In his absence, the two children had climbed on their mama's bed. Jace rubbed his chubby hand up and down Mrs. Wilson's arm, and Amelia patted her head. The woman slept on.

Daniel checked her forehead. The fever had risen again. "Amelia, I want you to carefully wring out this cloth." He held up the piece of petticoat from the night before. "Then run it over your mama's face and arms. Can you do that?"

She slipped her fingers into her mouth and nodded.

"You need to be very careful about her sore. Don't touch it, or wet her leg, okay?

The bed would probably be soaked when he returned, but he needed to change the sheet, anyway. Daniel watched for a few minutes as Amelia cooled her mama's body, amazed at how carefully the little girl dealt with the water. Very little actually dripped from the cloth. Jace watched his sister's every move.

Satisfied the little ones would be occupied for a time, Daniel grabbed a large heavy coat on a hook by the back door and headed out.

The weathered barn, where he'd hoped to sleep and be on his way, stood empty. With the number of stalls Mr. Wilson had built, there must have been three or four horses at one time. And most likely a milk cow. Now the entire building remained vacant, dust motes rising in the air as his boots kicked up the hay scattered on the floor of the structure.

The smokehouse also held nothing, however, two fat hens occupied the chicken coop. They must've been hidden in the woods when the *damn Rebs* took everything. He smiled. Even he had started to think of his comrades that way. He'd been on raids before his capture, but never would he leave a family with so little.

The garden would have been picked clean before the winter frost had set in. Hopefully, Mrs. Wilson had put up the vegetables before the raid. A grove of apple trees, their bare branches outlined by the blue sky, led to a cluster of pear trees. The farm had been healthy and productive at one time.

He wandered toward a large elm tree to where a wooden cross had been stuck in the ground.

Hans Wilson, b. May 22, 1821, d. November 11, 1864.

The head of the family had died a little over three months ago. When had the raid taken place? He'd heard rumors in prison that General Lee, and his army were holed up near the Virginia railroad station at Petersburg for over two hundred days. Would he have sent raiders this far north for supplies? As soon as he was able to leave, Daniel would make his way south, and join Lee's army. This could very well be the final push of the war. A war that had dragged on way too long.

He stopped and stared over the barren countryside. The fighting couldn't continue much longer. The Confederates had been the underdog from the start. Daniel hadn't remember seeing a single factory producing guns or ammunition anywhere in the south. Additionally, the southern railroads were small and not interconnected. But the main detriment was the South's reliance on tobacco and cotton, producing very little food to supply an entire army.

It seemed all the Rebs had was arrogance and pride.

Daniel sighed and returned to the problem at hand. One thing for certain, if he left now, the Wilson family would starve. As dangerous as his presence here continued to be, honor demanded he stay until assured of their well-being.

The first order of business remained food, followed by enough wood to keep the family warm for the rest of the winter. He headed to the back of the house to check the root cellar, which he'd heard all northern farmhouses had. A thorough search revealed a heavy wooden door built into the side of a small hill a short distance from the house.

The wood creaked and groaned as he pried the door open. A small oil lamp sat on the floor at the entrance, but he had no flint to light it. By opening the door all the way, the sun rays from outside allowed him to at least peer into the small room. Shelves lined the hard-packed dirt walls.

Praise the Lord, something the damn Rebs had missed.

Jars of fruits and vegetables sat in all their tempting glory. Daniel moved into the center of the room, his hands on his hips, as he surveyed his find. Corn, peas, green beans, tomatoes, applesauce, and pears. Numerous baskets on the floor held potatoes, carrots, squash, and dried apples. Onions and various herbs hung from hooks in the ceiling. This bounty must be how the family had survived since the husband died.

He emptied the contents of a half-filled basket of potatoes, and placed a jar of applesauce and a few potatoes, carrots, and an onion in it. One good shove with his shoulder, and the door closed. Juggling the jar and vegetables, he carried them to the kitchen.

Chandler sat at the wooden table cleaning the shotgun so recently pointed at Daniel's chest.

"How would you like to go hunting with me?" Daniel set the food down, keeping his eye on the gun and the boy's movements.

Chandler shrugged.

"We could get some fresh meat for the family." He pulled out a chair and sat next to him. "You know, Chandler, as the man of the family now, it's your job to make sure the family eats."

"I know that," he groused.

"Any luck?"

Chandler shook his head. Then he looked up at Daniel, the hostility gone, replaced by a child's fear. "Things were easier when Pa was here. I wanted him to teach me to hunt, but he always said, 'next year.'"

Daniel's heart twisted. What a burden for such a young boy.

"I'll tell you what. I'll check on your mama, and then once she's cleaned up and I'm sure she's doing all right, you and I will hunt up some dinner."

"Both of us?"

"Yes, son, both of us. You go ahead and finish your chore, and I'll check on your mama."

Daniel stood and stretched, wincing when he got a whiff of himself. A bath was definitely in order sometime soon. "Where does your mama keep the clean sheets?"

"I'll show you." Chandler jumped up from his seat, and hurried to a cabinet in the parlor. "Here." He pulled out a sheet, and brought it to Daniel.

"Maybe a clean pillow slip, too?"

The boy returned to the cabinet, and rifled around a bit before emerging with a white pillow slip, blue and purple embroidery carefully stitched along the hem.

"Thank you. Now you put that gun together, and once I take care of your mama, I'll be back and we'll go hunting."

"What about Jace and Amelia?"

"I think as long as they stay in your mama's room, they'll be all right until we return."

Gathering the sheet and pillow slip to his chest, Daniel headed down the hallway toward the bedroom where his patient lay.

The woman must have been awake, because a soft female voice reached his ears, along with the bright chatter of Amelia. Smiling, he entered the doorway.

Mrs. Wilson lay flat on her back, her two youngest children flanking either side. Her deep blue eyes glittered with anger. She rose up on one elbow, and with a shaky hand she raised a pistol, cocked, and aimed at his chest, just as he cleared the doorway.

"Get the hell out of my house, Reb."

CHAPTER THREE

"Don't shoot him, he's my friend." Amelia climbed off her mother's bed and ran to Daniel, wrapping her thin arms around his leg.

Once again, Daniel faced a gun pointed at his chest. He raised one hand as he laid the sheets and pillowslip on the chair next to the door. "Mrs. Wilson, my name is Lt. Daniel McCoy, and I'm not here to harm you or your family."

Her lips curled in a sneer. "That's what the last band of Confederate thieves said before they took every animal and bit of food they could find." She winced with pain as she changed positions. "If you don't figure starving a family is not doing them harm, then be on your way before I blow a hole in you."

He slowly lowered his hands, but kept them at his sides, palms facing outward. "Ma'am, I arrived yesterday in search of a drink of water and a place to bed down for the night. You and your children were in a bad way."

"In a bad way thanks to the Rebels." She attempted to steady the pistol with her other hand. "Amelia, move away from him."

"No, Mama. He made your leg all better. Now you

22

won't die." The little girl released one arm from his thigh and stuck her fingers in her mouth.

He kept his eye on the pistol shaking in the woman's hands. "I wasn't part of that raid, and I only want to help you before I'm on my way."

Losing the battle with the weight of the gun, Rosemarie dropped it to her side and closed her eyes. "Amelia tells me you're the one that fixed my leg."

"Yes, ma'am."

She opened her eyes, and two tears slid from their depths down her cheeks. "Thank you." The sound barely a whisper.

Daniel sucked in a deep breath and moved farther into the room. He knew how much those two words cost her. Mrs. Wilson was not the sort of woman who wanted to be beholding to anyone.

"I promise I'll only be here long enough to see you back on your feet." He nodded toward her leg. "You have a nasty cut there, and it will be some time before you're able to get around."

She wiped her eyes with the heels of her hands. "How is it you know so much about injuries, Reb?"

He bit back a grin at the name she continued to call him. "I worked as a medic in prison."

Her eyes widened, and she hugged Jace to her side. "Prison? Amelia, come back here. Now."

"Not regular prison," he hurried on. "The Yankees captured me, and sent me to Camp Morton in Indianapolis until a couple of weeks ago when I escaped."

Rosemarie collapsed against the pillow, all animation gone from her face. "Do what you have to, and go."

"I intended to change your sheet and check your bandage. Can I move you to the parlor while I do that?"

She shifted to rise, and let out a low keening sound.

"No. Don't move by yourself." Daniel strode across the room, took the gun from her side, and placed the weapon high on the shelf over her bed. Sliding his arms

23

underneath her body, he lifted her and the blanket at the same time.

The woman's face lost all color. She bit her lip and moaned softly against his chest. Mixed with the smell of the medicine he'd used, her faint scent of lemon swirled around him. Still warm from fever, her heat seeped through his worn shirt to his skin. He tried not to jar her as he moved to the parlor, where he gently laid her on the settee.

Amelia stood next to her mama, her eyes wide as she watched him.

"Amelia, can you fetch the blankets from the beds in your room, then bring them here to your mama?"

The child hurried away, brown curls bouncing down her back.

"As soon as I cut more wood, we'll have a fire. Right now I'll add the extra blankets and clean up your bed."

Rosemarie reached for his hand as he turned. "Why are you doing this? We're nobody to you. You're a Reb."

"I'm a man first. And you need looking after." He took the blankets from Amelia's hands and settled them around Rosemarie. Assured she would stay as warm as possible under the circumstances, he left the two children sitting near her.

Rosemarie's gaze followed the stranger as he left the room. A Rebel named Daniel McCoy, an escaped prisoner of war.

I can't believe things have gotten so bad I'm relying on the enemy to take care of me and my children.

No, not her enemy. Not her war, either. Hans had been adamant he would not leave his land to fight the Rebs, a bunch of devil-worshiping slave holders, as he called them.

The throbbing in her leg reminded her why she needed to keep her anger at the Reb in check. She was laid up, and he certainly looked as if he could handle the chores. Although Hans had been a large man, this Reb was bigger. Though most likely on the thin side because of his stint as a prisoner, his broad shoulders and large chest straining his filthy uniform left no doubt as to his ability to chop wood, plow a field, or swing a hammer. His dark brown hair hung to his chin, and his unshaven face gave him the look of a large bear. The entire time he spoke with her, he continued to push wayward strands of hair behind his ears.

His most remarkable feature, hazel eyes flecked with gold, radiated warmth and trust.

Ha. As if any Reb could be trusted.

No matter. She had no choice but to trust him. He'd saved her life, and hopefully, her leg as well. As grateful as she felt, her discomfort at his presence would not ease until she saw his back for the last time.

"Mama, why are you mad at my friend?" Amelia's blue eyes met hers.

"I'm not mad at him, honey. I think he's a very nice man for taking care of me while I'm sick."

"I know." Her eyes widened as she nodded. "And he made scrambled eggs so I didn't have to eat oatmeal."

Rosemarie smiled. She doubted Hans would have made scrambled eggs to keep the little girl happy. Although a hard worker and good provider, there had been nothing soft in her dead husband's nature. Definitely of the 'spare the rod and spoil the child' ilk, the only time his hands touched their children was when he spanked them. Not that he spanked them often. Good children by nature, they required little discipline. After the child's experience with men, Rosemarie found it amazing that Amelia seemed to accept the Reb so easily. It had been said that a child can sense goodness in a person.

"Mama, me and Mr. McCoy are going hunting today." Chandler entered the parlor, his eyes alight with wonder.

Rosemarie frowned. "Your papa didn't think you

were old enough to hunt yet."

Chandler nodded. "I know, but Mr. McCoy said as the man of the family now, I have to make sure everyone eats." He drew himself up, a sense of pride in his smile.

"That's right, son. You need to help your family with your pa gone." Daniel ruffled the boy's hair as he passed, and headed to the sofa. "Your bed is ready now, ma'am."

Once settled on the fresh sheet, a growing need in her lower parts had Rosemarie shifting on the bed.

Daniel watched her, his large hands on his hips. "Is your leg hurting? If I slip a pillow under it, the pain might ease a bit."

How to tell this stranger she needed the chamber pot? "Um, yes my leg hurts, but there's something else."

He waited for her to continue, his eyebrows raised.

"I, ah." She stiffened, and hitched her chin. "I need the chamber pot."

Daniel's lip twitched, but he quickly re-arranged his features. "Oh. Yes. I'm sorry. Where is it?"

She closed her eyes, wishing he would leave. "Under the bed."

He pulled out the pink and white flowered lidded bowl and handed the container to her. "I'll send Chandler in to help you."

Rosemarie took care of her business, and winced with pain as she climbed back into bed with her son's help. Chandler left her as she settled in.

A wave of exhaustion washed over her as she rested her head on the pillow. No matter how embarrassed she was, she had to let the Reb stay a day or so. She was tired. So very tired. Her eyes drifted closed

Several minutes after Chandler had returned from assisting his mother, Daniel tapped on the bedroom door. No answer. He opened the door, and peeked into the room. Rosemarie lay on the bed, eyes closed, her chest moving softly up and down. He moved closer and rested his hand on her forehead. The fever had returned, along with a slight flush to her cheeks.

"Is Ma okay?" Chandler stood outside the door, the rifle clutched in his hands.

"She's sleeping right now. Where are your brother and sister?"

"They're asleep on the settee in the parlor." He laid the gun on the floor. "Should I carry them in here to sleep with Ma?"

"No. Having them all together might seem like a good way to keep warm, but I'm afraid they might roll into your ma and hurt her leg."

"Ma keeps some extra blankets in there." He pointed to a long maple chest at the foot of Rosemarie's bed.

"Good. Fetch a couple of blankets to cover Amelia and Jace. Then you and I are going hunting."

Chandler raced to do as he asked.

Daniel covered Rosemarie, and studied her for a moment. So delicate, how in hell could she keep the farm going alone? Despite her paleness and the dark circles under her eyes, Rosemarie was a pretty woman.

A rosebud mouth, high cheekbones, and dark lashes rested against her fever-flushed cheeks. The long braid of brown and gold silky hair had loosened. Wouldn't she be surprised to have him offer to brush and re-braid her hair? He'd oftentimes done that for his mother when she suffered one of her headaches.

His mind drifted to the memory of Maggie McCoy, his mother, and how overcome with anger he'd been when he visited his family's horse ranch a couple of years ago. His regiment's march through Virginia had given him the opportunity to stop by his homestead.

He was stunned to learn his mother had sold the McCoy land—his birthright. He'd tracked her down to a decrepit boarding house where she was living out her last days, suffering from consumption. It didn't take much for him to forgive her when she'd explained how with both sons gone, she had to sell the land to pay the taxes. The tiny bit left from the sale barely kept a roof over her head and food in her stomach.

Realizing what little thought he and his brother had given their mother's welfare when they'd both rushed off to war, he was consumed with guilt.

He'd held her hand, and kissed her dry cheek before returning to the battle. Knowing it was the last time he'd see her, he left her bedside with tears standing in his eyes. His land had been sold, his mother hovered near death, and his brother was fighting with the enemy. It had taken weeks of interminable marches and battles in bitter cold to numb his spirit to the losses he'd suffered.

He shoved the thoughts to the back of his mind and joined Chandler, who waited impatiently on the porch. They headed down the steps, the rifle clutched in Daniel's hand.

Once behind the cleared area of the house and the grove of pear and apple trees, they entered a heavily wooded section. Thick branches from large elm and oak trees blocked the meager winter sun.

"What kind of animals are we huntin'?" Chandler skipped alongside him, his warm breath visible in the cold air.

"Since it's late in the day, I think we'll be lucky to get a couple of rabbits." He smiled at the boy. "Do you like rabbit stew?"

"Yes, sir. Mama fixes that a lot. Pa used to bring home heaps of rabbits."

"What else did he hunt?"

"Deer, mostly. Once he shot a pig, but Ma said it probably belonged to Mr. Macey, and got mad when Pa wouldn't return it."

Daniel smiled at the bit of family gossip. What had Hans Wilson been like? Based on what he'd calculated from the man's grave marker, he'd been forty-three when he died. Even with the haggard look from her illness,

Rosemarie had to be no more than twenty-four or five.

Chandler turned and walked backwards, skipping along as only a child could do. "Mr. McCoy, why do you have slaves?"

"I don't have slaves, never did."

"Pa said all Rebs had slaves, and beat and starved them."

Daniel grabbed the boy's shoulder before he walked into a small birch tree. "Not all southerners have slaves. My family owned a horse ranch in Virginia for many years, and we never had even one slave."

"You calling my pa a liar?" Chandler's back stiffened.

Daniel sighed and squatted in front of the boy. "No, not a liar, but misinformed."

Chandler's eyes narrowed. "What's that mean?"

Daniel took his hat off, ran his fingers through his hair, then settled it back on his head. "Some people in the south have slaves, mostly those who have large plantations."

Chandler's brows drew together. "What's a plantation?"

"Like a farm, but very big. Most people in the south don't have slaves, don't want them, and couldn't afford to buy one if they wanted to." He placed his hand on the child's shoulder and rose. "The Confederacy is not fighting for slaves, although that's part of it. We're fighting for state's rights."

"What's that mean?"

"It means we don't want the Federal government, the people in Washington, telling us in Virginia how to live, what to do."

"You a teacher, Mr. McCoy?"

Daniel smiled. "No."

Chandler shrugged. "You sure sound like one."

Side by side, they continued on for a while, the cold air reddening their cheeks. Chandler glanced up at Daniel. "Do you miss your pa, and your horse ranch?"

Daniel shrugged and turned to the boy. "My pa's dead. So's my ma. And with me and my brother gone off to war, she had to sell the horse farm."

Chandler digested the information, then said, "Does that make you feel sad?"

He smiled at the concern on the young boy's face. "Yes. I do feel sad. But a man has to move on when things don't go the way he wants."

"I have an idea," Chandler said, his eyes lighting up. "You can stay here with us, and take care of Ma and our farm."

Daniel winced at the hope in the boy's eyes. "Staying here does sound like a good idea, son, but we're in the middle of a war, and I have to return to my regiment. Once your ma is feeling better, I'll have to leave."

"My pa said he wouldn't leave his family to fight a bunch of slave-loving Rebs."

Daniel chuckled and shook his head. "Well, your pa had a family to provide for. I don't."

"We can be your family." The words came out soft and hesitant, his young eyes filled with hope.

Before he could answer, Chandler tugged on Daniel's cuff. Then he pointed off in the distance. "Rabbits."

Several rabbits stood still, only their whiskers twitching. A rabbit den must be close by. Daniel raised his index finger to his lips and shook his head.

Chandler nodded his understanding and stood perfectly still. After studying the small animals, Daniel bent on one knee and raised the firearm, aiming for the largest one. A quick shot scattered the group of rabbits, and the largest one lay on the ground, blood seeping from its head.

"You got 'em!" Chandler shouted, and raced to where the animal lay. He picked the body up, and held the dripping carcass out, a bright smile on his face.

Daniel slung the rifle over his shoulder and joined him.

"Are we gonna shoot some more?" the boy asked,

jumping up and down.

"Not today, son. I'm a little nervous with your ma back there all alone with the two little ones."

"Oh, that's right." Chandler grinned. "We're the men, and we have to protect them."

Daniel ruffled the boy's hair. "Indeed we do. It's our job to make sure the women-folk are safe."

Why did his comment feel so good? He'd always known one day he would have a wife and hopefully a family. He shook his head at his foolishness. The boy's words had affected him. Now was certainly not the time, nor place, to be thinking along those lines. He needed to remove himself from enemy territory and re-join his regiment. Besides, Rosemarie Wilson despised him, and most likely would fill him full of buckshot if he wasn't gone in a few days.

He grinned. The best part of this whole package would be that fiery woman confined to bed. She was all spit and vinegar, but the softness in her seeped out when she dealt with her children. Had her husband seen that soft side too? It was too bad he couldn't stick around to find out.

In fact, given the attraction he was beginning to feel, he best beat a path as far away from her as possible.

CHAPTER FOUR

Daniel slapped the gutted rabbit on the table and hung the rifle over the fireplace. "I'm gonna check on your ma. Can you go out back to the few hens left and collect whatever eggs are there?"

Chandler nodded and raced out the door.

Rosemarie tossed on the bed, her mass of brown and gold hair tangling as she moved. Daniel approached the bed and checked her forehead for fever. It had spiked again.

"Hans?" Her voice barely rose above a whisper.

"No, Rosemarie. It's Daniel."

Her brow furrowed. "Thirsty."

"Give me a minute to bring you something to drink, and to cool you down. I'll be right back." He touched his fingertips to her arm, and she stopped moving. Her dry skin seeped heat into his fingers.

After retrieving the pan of water from the floor, he strode down the hallway to the kitchen.

Chandler added eggs to the bowl from the pocket he'd made with the front of his shirt. "How's Ma?"

"Her fever's returned. I'll have to bathe her again." Daniel pumped fresh water into the pan and glanced over his shoulder. "Can you see to your brother and sister when they wake up?"

Chandler frowned. "What about the rabbit?"

"I don't suppose you know how to skin it?"

The boy shook his head, his face paling. "No. Ma always did that stuff."

"All right, I'll do it when I'm finished with your ma." He nodded in the direction of the basket sitting on the floor. "Why don't you wash those vegetables and set them into a pot of water? We'll add the rabbit in a little bit."

Daniel grabbed the cloths left to dry next to the sink, then carefully carried the pan of water down the hall. As he reached the doorway, he turned and spoke in a loud whisper. "Bring your ma a glass of water, please?" Then he ducked under the door jamb and headed to the bed.

Tears slid down Rosemarie's cheeks. When the bed dipped as he sat alongside her, she opened her eyes. "Where are my children?"

"Chandler is fetching you a glass of water. Jace and Amelia are asleep in the parlor."

"What are you doing here? I thought I told you to leave." Her sore lips barely moved. He had to bend close to her mouth to hear what she whispered.

"You people sure know how to welcome visitors."

Her lips twitched.

"You need help, ma'am, and your children require someone to watch over them while you're laid up."

"Ma?" Chandler stood alongside the bed, glass in hand. "Do you feel better?"

She nodded and reached for the water.

Daniel slid his hand under her head, and eased her up so she could drink.

"Not too much," he said after she'd taken a few sips.

She handed the glass back to Chandler. "You taking care of your brother and sister?" Rosemarie's voice had eased with the water.

"Yeah. And me and Mr. McCoy shot a rabbit."

33

Chandler's chest puffed out, his mouth in a wide grin.

Rosemarie's gaze swung to Daniel. "Where's the rifle now?"

Before Daniel could answer, Chandler jumped in. "Mr. McCoy put it away—up high over the fireplace, so's the little ones can't reach it."

Rosemarie closed her eyes and nodded.

"All right, son, why don't you leave that water there, on the dresser, and check on Jace and Amelia while I cool your ma off."

Daniel slid the sheet down, then dipped the cloth into the water. With great care, he bathed her heated body with the water, trying to ignore her full curves.

"I hate Rebels." She spoke with her eyes still closed.

"I know. And ma'am, for what it's worth, I hate what they did to you, too."

She moved her head and opened her deep blue eyes. "You're one of them."

He shook his head and wrung out the cloth. "No, ma'am. I'm a Confederate soldier, but not one of the men who stole everything from you."

The clock ticked in the background for a minute before she spoke. "Not yet, anyway."

He smiled at the slight tilt of her lips.

The next morning, Daniel carried his cup of chicory-laced coffee to the front porch and settled on the top step. He took a sip, grateful it wasn't plain chicory, which was all he'd had to drink practically since the war had started. He and Rosemarie had declared a truce for as long as she needed his help. He grinned at her sassy attitude, despite being bedridden. She continued to call him "Reb," but some of the disdain had gone from her voice.

The sun crept over the hill in the distance, slowly removing any trace of the dusky dawn—his favorite time of day. He inhaled deeply, but the cold winter air of Indiana didn't soothe him. Before the war had taken over his life, he'd sat on his front porch just about every morning in Virginia, coffee in hand, readying himself for the day.

Days spent training horses and caring for them. Working on his own land where he'd been born and had expected to die. He'd thought to spend the rest of his life repeating those days, eventually marrying one of the young ladies from the county, having a passel of kids. The horse farm had been his life, his legacy, in his family since his great grandfather, Sean McCoy, had stepped off the ship from Ireland and earned enough money to buy his first few horses.

Then the war came, and after days of heated arguments over the dinner table, his brother decided to honor their mother's people, who were from nearby West Virginia, by signing on with the Union Army. Maggie had been proud, Daniel disgusted. What he'd seen as Stephen's betrayal had caused a break in their lifelong friendship that might never be healed. He took another sip of the warming beverage and rubbed the back of his neck.

Where was his younger brother now? Had he been killed in battle? Wounded? He might never know. Once the ire had subsided at what he'd considered his brother's betrayal, a gnawing fear for the younger man's life took the anger's place, never to diminish during all the years of the war. Even fighting against each other wouldn't break the brothers' bond.

"Mr. a'Coy, whatcha doing out here?" Amelia's soft baby voice interrupted his musings.

He turned to smile at the little girl, face flushed from sleep, dragging a rag doll behind her.

"Just enjoying the sunrise, darlin'."

She settled alongside him, snuggling into the warmth of his body.

He placed his arm around her thin shoulders and pulled her close. "You shouldn't be out here without your coat."

"I forgot." She tucked her fingers into her mouth,

and regarded him wide-eyed. "Are we goin' to have oatmeal for breakfast again?"

"No, ma'am. Chandler brought in some more eggs yesterday, and we'll scramble 'em up for you."

She nodded. "Good. I like scrambled eggs."

Daniel stood, scooping Amelia into his arms. "It's time to start breakfast, and I need to check on your ma."

Amelia yawned, tiny tears forming in her eyes. "She's sleeping. 'Cause I just looked."

He deposited her on the chair as Chandler entered the kitchen, rubbing his eyes. "Why were you outside?"

"Looking at the beautiful sunrise," Daniel said as he ruffled Chandler's hair. "Why don't you fetch those eggs you collected yesterday and scramble 'em up while I see to your ma?"

"And don't make oatmeal, Chandler." Amelia's voice drifted down the hall as he headed to Rosemarie's bedroom.

She lay on her side, the sore leg balanced on a pillow, just as he'd left her the night before.

"Good morning." He approached the bed as her eyes opened. "How do you feel?"

"The leg pains me, but I don't think I have a temperature anymore." Her eyes, no longer glazed with fever, watched him as he felt her forehead.

"Nice and cool. You're right."

Rosemarie shifted, and winced. "Can you help me sit? I'm sore from lying in the same position all night."

Daniel fluffed pillows behind her, and then reached his arm around to pull her up to a sitting position, carefully leaning her against the headboard.

Her face paled, and she bit her lip.

"I'm sorry, I tried not to move your leg too much."

She took in a deep breath. "It's all right. I have to get up today anyway."

Daniel rested his hands on his hips. "I don't think so."

"Excuse me?" Her chin rose, and her eyes flashed in defiance.

"I don't mean to tell you what to do, but it's really not a good idea to get out of bed yet."

"Look, Reb, I have work to do, children to take care of."

"That's why I'm here, ma'am. I can stay for a few days until you're on your feet again." He pointed at her leg. "You could rip those stitches out, and you'd be back where you started."

"Won't the army be looking for you?"

Daniel nodded. "Most likely both sides. But I won't leave until I know you can handle things."

She closed her eyes. "Why?"

Even though she couldn't see, he shrugged. "I wouldn't be much of a man if I left you in this condition, with three little ones to care for."

"We're not your concern." She raised her eyelids and peered at him.

His jaw tightened. "You are now."

"Mama, Jace wet the bed again, and Chandler's mad. He said he's gonna make me eat oatmeal, even though Mr. a'Coy said he would cook me scrambled eggs. He's being mean." Amelia climbed on the bed, and Daniel grabbed her when he saw Rosemarie's face pale.

"Best to stay off your mama's bed until her leg is better." He shifted Amelia in his arms, and glanced at Rosemarie . "Can you wait until I settle the kids with breakfast before I tend to you?"

"Take care of them, I'll be fine."

Rosemarie studied the large man as he left the room carrying her little girl, her arms wrapped tightly around his neck.

He's a Reb.

It would do her well to remember that. The southern scoundrels took all their food, shot her husband, and left him for dead. Even with the best nursing she'd ever done, Hans had succumbed within days. And she'd been left alone with three young children.

Since then, not a day passed that she didn't feel the burning of hatred in her stomach. At one time, she'd been a contented—if not happy—wife and mother, and within days she stood alone, struggling to keep her children from starving.

The Rebs had taken her animals, including the horses. With winter upon them, and no way to visit any of the surrounding farms to solicit help, she and her eight-year-old son had dug her husband's grave while the two little ones watched in confused silence. She'd conducted the burial service herself, praying from the worn Bible Hans had brought with him from Germany.

After a supper of soup and bread, she had put the children to bed. Then she sat in the rocking chair Hans had made, and rocked, a blanket wrapped around her shaking body. Her eyes were still wide open and dry when the sun peeked over the horizon and flooded the bedroom she'd shared with her husband for nine years. A man she hadn't really known.

Now another large man had entered her life. One as unwanted and unwelcomed as Hans had been. Only this large man had gentle hands when he wiped her down with cool water. He carried Amelia in his arms and made her scrambled eggs because she didn't like oatmeal. He took Chandler hunting, and didn't push the boy aside and tell him he was too young.

She winced as she moved again, trying to ease her sore bottom. Despite what the Reb said, she would be up today, and back to her work in a day or so. The children were already too attached to him. A man who smiled at them, rather than frowned.

But a Confederate escaped prisoner.

It also annoyed her at how her heart sped up when he looked at her with those piercing hazel eyes. And the tilt of his lips when he began to smile. Just her luck to be attracted to a southern Rebel wanted by the Union Army. Thank God he'd be gone soon.

"Careful you don't drop it." The Reb's deep voice rolled over her as he and Amelia entered the bedroom. Jace toddled behind them, then raced for her bed when he spotted her. McCoy scooped him up before he landed on her leg, and tossed him over his shoulder, causing the child to giggle and shriek.

Amelia carried a tray with a cup of tea and a bowl of oatmeal. She never looked up as she approached the bed, keeping her eyes on the tray. "Mama, I brought you breakfast."

"I see that, Amelia. How nice of you." Rosemarie's heart melted at the sight of her little girl carefully walking across the room.

The child's face broke into a smile as she reached her mama's side. "Whew," she sighed as she placed the tray on the table next to Rosemarie's bed.

"Good job, Amelia. You remembered to not place the tray on your mama's bed."

Amelia puffed her chest out. "I remembered." Then she slid her fingers into her mouth.

Jace reached his arms out. "Mama."

"Let me eat my breakfast, and then you can sit on my lap." Rosemarie reached for the cup of tea and sipped as the Reb juggled a red-faced Jace. The baby was having none of it, and let out a wail.

Rosemarie returned the teacup to the table and stretched her arms out. "I can eat while he sits on my lap."

Daniel handed over Jace, who cuddled up to her, burrowing his nose into her generous breasts. She glanced up at Daniel, her face heated at the look in his eyes.

Lucky kid.

Daniel smiled to himself as he watched Jace nuzzling Rosemarie. The clarity in her eyes denied the flush on her face came from fever. The little guy had embarrassed her. He bit his lip to keep from smiling. Somehow he didn't think she would appreciate knowing his thoughts. "When you're finished with your breakfast, ma'am, I'll want to take a look at your injury, be sure it's still healing."

She nodded and reached for the bowl of oatmeal.

He turned to leave when she called him. "Reb?"

"The name's Daniel, ma'am."

"If you want to change, there are clean clothes you can use, hanging on the nails in the mudroom. They were my husband's and might fit you."

Daniel nodded. "Thank you, I appreciate it. Is there a creek nearby where I can wash up?"

"About half a mile east of the house, but it'll be mighty cold this time of year."

"No matter. I'll take those clothes you offered and head to the creek." He nodded and left the room.

Daniel plucked a soft flannel shirt and worn wool pants from the nail, grabbed a linen cloth from a small pile on the table underneath, and headed to the kitchen. There he took a small brown jug containing lye soap and left the house.

Although different from his homestead, this section of Indiana had an appeal all its own. Consisting mostly of rolling forests and prairie, the area provided good, rich farmland. It appeared the Wilson farm provided plenty of food to sustain the family, along with several acres of corn, which most likely brought in cash.

Hans had built the house to withstand the heat of summer and the cold winds of winter. The structure sat nestled between several large oaks, which would provide plenty of cooling protection from strong summer sunlight.

Sturdy shutters framed each window, which boasted much coveted panes of glass. All in all, the farm looked solid and productive—a place that could easily add horse breeding to its design.

Get your mind off that subject. This is all temporary for you.

Had it not been for the war, he would certainly stick around to see if this attraction he felt for Rosemarie was something permanent. And discover if she felt it, too. Running his palms over her soft, curvy body as he cooled her down, had transferred the heat from her body to his. But he needed to put those thoughts aside.

Daniel whistled as he surveyed the area, and made his way to the creek. After scrubbing his body and hair, then rubbing the goose bumps on his skin dry, he tugged on the pants, which were a bit loose in the waist. He switched his suspenders from his worn uniform to the wool pants. The flannel shirt stretched across his chest, straining the buttons. The cuffs were a bit short, so he rolled them to his elbows. Hans Wilson had been a large man, but not quite as large as Daniel.

After gathering his filthy uniform, he bundled the pieces, strode off into the woods, and buried them under a log. Checking the pocket of the borrowed pants to assure himself the ring was there, Daniel headed back to the house, feeling and smelling a whole lot better than when he'd left.

Daniel spent the next couple of days working on the chicken coop that had fallen into disrepair since Hans' passing. Then he and the three children scoured the woods, rounding up the escaped chickens and returning them to their proper home. He fixed part of a fence that had blown down during a winter storm.

He tried to avoid touching Rosemarie as much as possible. Amelia had been designated to fetch and carry for her, but Daniel still found himself drawn to her room, even for just conversation. And a few times a day, he gathered her warm body into his arms and carried her to the kitchen for meals, or to the parlor for a change of scenery.

It was these times that he knew he had to rein in his feelings, and remember who he was, and where he was.

Nothing could come of this attraction they both felt. He'd see it in her eyes when he glanced at her while her face flushed an enticing pink.

Late one afternoon, after gathering onions, potatoes, and carrots from the storage cellar, he dumped them onto the kitchen table. The chicken he'd killed lay alongside the vegetables, everything ready for someone to fix the meal. Daniel stood, hands on his hips, studying the items. Cooking for a family had never been one of his better skills. He'd managed to put together beans and rice for supper, as well as a potato and onion soup. But this was beyond him.

His head snapped up at the sound of a thud coming from the bedroom.

"What was that?" Chandler frowned from where he worked on sums Rosemarie had assigned him.

"I don't know," Daniel shot over his shoulder as he strode down the hallway to Rosemarie's bedroom.

She sat on the floor, leaning against the bed, her face stark white, eyes pinched closed in pain.

"What are you doing?" Daniel hunkered down alongside her.

"I have to get up and get some work done. I'm sick to death of lying in this bed." She spoke through clenched teeth.

He sat back on his heels. "So you were attempting to climb out of bed and stroll down the hallway to the kitchen? Or maybe to the mudroom to do some washing? Or perhaps—"

"Stop." She opened her eyes, dark with anger. "I'm not stupid. I merely tried to sit on the edge of the bed, and I slipped." She blew out a puff of air, fluttering the curls resting on her forehead.

He'd spent a good hour yesterday washing her hair in the kitchen sink, then combing it and re-braiding the silky locks. She'd thanked him, blushing furiously when she told him no one had ever done that for her before. She was such a sweet woman, and deserved so much more than she'd gotten in life. Had things been different, he would like to be the man who would give her what she'd missed.

Daniel stood and crossed his arms over his chest. He looked down at her. "If you really want to get up and help, maybe I can carry you to the kitchen, and you can do something with that food sitting on the table."

She nodded and shifted. "I can do that."

He bent and swept her into his arms, noting the wince as he settled her. "Sorry."

"It's fine."

Her body slid against his, warm and smooth. Daniel broke into a sweat as the soft pillows of her breasts pressed against his chest. The female scent of her drifted to his nostrils, causing his stomach muscles to clench. What the devil was wrong with him?

A mother of three, on her deathbed only a few days ago, and I'm constantly riddled with lusty thoughts?

Obviously, he'd been without a woman too long.

He settled her on a chair in front of the mound of vegetables. Rosemarie's teeth clamped down on her lips, and paled as she adjusted her leg.

After taking a deep breath, she turned to Chandler. "Can you bring my dressing gown from the bottom of my bed?"

"I'll build up a fire in the stove. That will help to warm you." Daniel headed to the back door.

"There isn't much wood left."

"There's plenty," he answered as the back door slammed.

His gut twisted as he strode to the pile of wood he'd cut earlier. He didn't like where his thoughts were going. In no time at all, the three Wilson children had crawled into his heart. Those feelings he could deal with, but his growing awareness of Rosemarie disturbed him. He had a duty to the Confederacy. He had a regiment to return to, a war to fight.

43

And in case you forgot, the Union army is looking for you, too. You'd better ignore that sassy woman who smells so good, and whose body is so soft and warm. Do what you can to help her, and then leave.

CHAPTER FIVE

Rosemarie blew out the breath she held. Why in heaven's name had her heart fluttered when the Reb carried her to the kitchen? A man's touch had never affected her that way before. Hans had taken her in the dark, pushing her nightgown up, groping for a bit, then shoving himself inside her. Never tender in his dealings with her or anyone else, she'd assumed his behavior to be true of all men.

Gruffness had been her experience with her father, too. Franz Bergmann had barely tolerated his ten children. He'd sent Rosemarie off to work in the house of Oliver P. Morton when she was barely thirteen. Now Governor of Indiana, Morton was then a well-known lawyer and former circuit judge. She'd spent two years there, doing laundry and cleaning, until her father arrived one day to announce she was to be married. Within days, he'd handed her to Hans. In payment of a debt. Papa got two horses, and Hans got a wife less than half his age.

But the Reb's touch had shaken her. The way he ran the cool cloth over her skin, with gentle strokes, to reduce her fever, how he ruffled Chandler's hair, and looked Amelia in the eye when he dealt with her. He used his large hands to sooth, and comfort.

And yesterday he'd washed her hair, massaging her scalp in a way that had goose bumps breaking out all over her body. Then, as if he was not the huge, strong man that he was, he proceeded to comb out her hair and re-braid it. The tenderness he showed her almost brought her to tears.

She stopped her thoughts. No point in getting attached to the Reb. He'd only be with them for a couple more days at the most.

The door slammed and Daniel carried in a stack of wood. She smiled. He'd been busy with more than scrambling eggs for Amelia and teaching Chandler how to hunt.

What would it be like to belong to a man such as Lt. Daniel McCoy? To know he would always care for her and her children. Show them tenderness, love and caring. Something her little family had been short of with her husband.

After stirring the embers of the stove, he shoved smaller pieces of wood in, then added two large logs. "This will warm things up for you."

"If you will wash these vegetables, and then hand me the small knife from the top drawer, I'll start fixing the stew." She shrugged into her dressing gown, wrapping it around her chilled body, and tied the belt securely.

Daniel quickly ran the food under the water pump, and set it before her. "Do you want me to remove the feathers from the chicken?"

Rosemarie looked at him in surprise. "I know how to pluck a bird."

He pulled out a chair, and sat next to her. "I'm sure you do. But I figure if we work together, it will go faster." He shot her a bright smile, and her blood heated up.

They worked side by side in silence for several minutes. His strong hands, dusted with brown hairs, drew her gaze as his fingers tugged on the feathers. What would those fingers feel like, cupping her chin, skimming over her breasts, touching her woman's parts? She shivered.

He frowned as he regarded her. "Are you still cold?"

"No. I'm fine." She lowered her head and concentrated on her work.

What in heaven's name was wrong with her, anyway? She laughed to herself at these wayward thoughts. Hadn't she had enough of men?

The front door slammed shut, and Chandler stood before her, his eyes wide. "Ma, there's a bunch of soldiers riding up."

"Rebs?" she asked, her heart speeding up.

"No, ma'am. Yankees."

Her gaze slid to Daniel, whose lips had tightened into a thin, white line.

They had obviously come to search for Daniel. He was an escaped prisoner. But, she reminded herself, a prisoner of war. Not her war. She continued to study him as she chewed her lip.

What must he be thinking? One shout from her and he would be caught, dragged back to prison to face who knew what. His piercing eyes never left her face as thoughts raced around her mind like the small circular wind storms they sometime had in the spring.

Before she could change her mind, she took a deep breath. "You must hide."

With those three words she sealed her fate. She would not turn the Reb—Daniel—in.

Not giving herself time to over-think her decision, she turned to Chandler. "Go to the porch and tell the soldiers your mama is ill. Perhaps they'll leave." Then she eyed Daniel. "In the mudroom is a small rug. Underneath is a trap door leading to a tunnel my husband dug years ago when Indian problems plagued the area. Hide in there." Her words tumbled out one on top of another.

Daniel stood and cupped her cheek, his eyes questioning.

"Go!"

He headed to the back of the house, and Chandler

raced for the front door.

"Wait," Rosemarie shouted at Chandler. "Come back here for a minute."

Her son returned to her side.

"Go cover the trapdoor with the rug once Mr. McCoy is down there. If the soldiers insist on coming into the house, go to the back bedroom, and stay there with Jace and Amelia. If they awake, keep them quiet, so as not to attract attention. Should they search the house, don't let your brother and sister say anything about Mr. McCoy."

"We're not gonna let them take him, are we?"

"No."

Chandler nodded and hurried to the door.

Rosemarie placed her hand on her chest, attempting to still her thumping heart. She tried to tell herself the soldiers could be scouring the land for provisions for the army. She couldn't afford to lose any more food.

Although she tried to continue with her vegetables, the knife in her shaky hands nicked one of her fingers, causing blood to drip on the table. Quickly, she wrapped the wound in her apron just as a loud male voice drifted from the porch.

"Tell your ma to come to the door."

Her flesh broke into goose bumps. The deep raspy voice sounded close enough to be in the next room. Had they already entered the house?

"Ma's sick. She can't walk real good."

"It's okay, Chandler. Let the men in." No point in hiding in the kitchen. The soldiers would do whatever they wanted anyway.

A large man, dressed in a dusty Yankee uniform, removed his cap as he ducked his head and stepped into the kitchen. His full red beard and mustache made it appear as if his face was on fire. Icy blue eyes without a drop of softness stared at her. He slowly ran his gaze from her face to her leg, wrapped in pieces of petticoat and resting on a small stool.

"Sorry to disturb you, ma'am." He moved closer, causing Rosemarie's breathing to accelerate. Behind him the clatter of booted heels preceded the arrival of several soldiers who crowded in behind their leader. "I'd like to speak with your husband."

She raised her chin and glared at him. "My husband is dead."

"Sorry." He gave her a curt nod.

"What can I do for you, Sergeant?" She didn't know his rank, but had to address him in some manner.

"It's Captain, ma'am. Captain Nelson." He stretched his lips—it could hardly be called a smile—and rested his hands on his hips.

She dipped her head in acknowledgement. "What can I do for you, Captain Nelson?"

Without receiving an invitation, he pulled out a chair and lowered his bulk into it. One soldier wandered around the kitchen, opening drawers, then pushed the curtain aside on the small window above the sink. Another stood behind the Captain, leering at her.

Rosemarie tensed, and gulped at the bile that rose to the back of her throat. Her sweaty palm smoothed the loose hair from her face.

Dear God. Please keep Amelia and Jace asleep in their beds. If they awake, the sight of the soldiers will terrify them, and keeping them quiet will be difficult for Chandler.

"We're looking for an escaped Rebel. Left Camp Morton a few weeks ago. We have reason to believe he's in the area, and dangerous."

She stiffened her spine and sniffed. "Indeed? And why are you troubling my family with this?"

"Well, ma'am, we're thinkin' for him to stay so well hidden, someone must be helpin' him."

"Someone could be helping him, if he was indeed in this area. Maybe you're wrong and he's long gone."

Captain Nelson removed his hat, ran dirty fingers through his wiry hair, and replaced the cap. "We traced him this far, but it doesn't appear he left the region."

"Maybe he's dead."

"Maybe. And maybe not. Either way, nobody escapes when I'm in charge. I take it as a personal affront." He stared in her eyes, not flinching, until she broke contact and picked up a vegetable. Noticing her shaking hands, she dropped it back onto the table.

"What happened to your leg?"

"I cut it while chopping wood." She raised her chin. "The Rebs came through here and took everything we had, and shot my husband. He died of his injury a few days later."

"I'm sorry to hear that ma'am." The captain tugged on the brim of his hat. "How you gettin' around, and takin' care of things with a cut leg?"

"We manage."

"Where's the boy what answered the door? He don't seem big enough to do much for ya."

Rosemarie ran her sweaty palm down the front of her apron. "He's in the back bedroom. My two little ones are asleep in there. Please don't disturb them."

Captain Nelson turned to the soldier leaning against the sink, and gestured with his chin toward the back of the house. "Go check."

Rosemarie held her breath as the soldier opened her bedroom door first, then the children's door. Since no sound came from the bedroom, Jace and Amelia must have remained asleep. She let out the breath she held when the soldier closed the door and returned to the kitchen.

"Just as she said, Captain, three kids in there. Two asleep and the bigger one sitting on the bed with them."

"Get the kid out here."

"No." Rosemarie's sharp reply caused all the soldiers to look in her direction.

The Captain regarded her with raised eyebrows. "Why not?"

"My little girl is sickly. If she awakes and her brother

isn't there, and she sees all these soldiers, she'll be frightened."

"There ain't nothin' to be scared of, ma'am." He narrowed his eyes. "Unless you got something to hide."

Unable to form words in her dry mouth, she merely shook her head.

"Go get the kid."

Rosemarie's heart beat so loudly, surely the men could hear it. She dropped her gaze to her lap as Chandler came into the room, the soldier behind him.

"Come here, boy." Captain Nelson extended his arm.

Chandler slowly walked to him, but stood next to Rosemarie. "What?"

"You seen any Rebel soldiers around here lately?"

He gave Rosemarie a quick glance, then shook his head.

"If ya did, ya'd tell me, wouldn't ya?" The Captain leaned forward and rested his elbows on his thighs, stabbing the boy with his eyes.

"Yes, sir."

"You know the Rebels are your enemy, ain't that right, boy? They would slit your throat while you sleep."

The boy's eyes grew wide, but he remained silent.

"And you ain't seen no strange men around?"

Chandler shook his head again.

The Captain stared at Chandler for a minute, then leaned back in the chair and nodded to Rosemarie . "How you get that leg taken care of?"

"My son helped."

"That right, boy?" The Captain again turned his attention to Chandler.

"Yes, sir."

"You cleaned that up for your ma, and wrapped it?"

Chandler looked at his feet, his face pale.

"Well?"

"Yes, sir."

The Captain glared at Rosemarie . "The soldier we're

lookin' for, who escaped from prison, was a medic." He tilted the legs of his chair back.

Rosemarie shrugged, and pulled Chandler closer to her side.

"You know if you're hidin' an escaped prisoner of war, you'd be in a heap of trouble."

"Captain, if you and your men are through with me and my family, I would appreciate you being on your way." She winced when she shifted in her seat. "I don't want my younger children to wake up and find you here."

A soldier she hadn't seen before entered the kitchen and walked up to the Captain. He didn't seem to be much older than Chandler. Peach fuzz on his face and adolescent pimples marked him as not much more than a boy. "Nothing, sir."

Captain Nelson addressed the young soldier, but kept his eyes on Rosemarie. "You check the barn and root cellar?"

"Yes, sir."

The Captain stood and shoved the chair under the table. "We'll be on our way, ma'am." He slung his rifle over his shoulder and leaned toward her. "I sure hope we don't have no reason to come back here."

He nodded and turned to leave, when a shout came from outside the house. Rosemarie's heart sped up once more. Had they found Daniel?

"Captain." Another young soldier dashed into the kitchen, his eyes wild. "Someone just took off with my horse."

"What the hell..." Captain Nelson pushed the soldier aside and strode to the door, the rest of the men following.

Rosemarie cursed her sore leg and her inability to see the activity outside the house. "Chandler, go to the porch and see what's going on."

Chandler dashed after the soldiers, the door banging behind him.

Rosemarie attempted to rise, but fell back when the

pain in her leg caused a wave of nausea to roll over her. Sweat broke out on her forehead and she slumped in the chair. Shouting, and the sound of horses galloping brought her attention to the kitchen window, where several soldiers, Captain Nelson in the lead, raced past the house.

Chandler hurried into the kitchen, his eyes wide. "I think Mr. McCoy got away."

Why did she feel like she'd been deserted—again? She mentally slapped herself. What did she expect, that Daniel would stay forever and solve all her problems?

She had a farm to run, and three children to feed. She didn't need his help or anyone else's for that matter. Her leg would heal, and everything would return to the way it was before the blighter entered her life. Good riddance. He made her feel uncomfortable anyway, the way his eyes lit up when he looked at her.

The way he made scrambled eggs for Amelia.

Well, goddammit, she could scramble eggs, too. She used her knuckle to wipe the tear from the piece of dirt that must've gotten into her eye. "Chandler, check the trapdoor—see if Mr. McCoy is gone."

Rosemarie held her hand to her throat as Chandler ran to the mudroom, and lifted the trap door. He climbed down, leaving the rapid beating of her heart the only sound in the room.

After a few minutes, Chandler's head poked up from the opening. "He's gone."

Rosemarie blew out the lamp in the kitchen, and leaning on the stick Chandler had found for her, hobbled to the bedroom. Close to midnight, and the three children were finally asleep.

She had a heck of a time explaining to Jace and Amelia why Daniel had left and would not be back again. It tore her up to see the look of disappointment on Amelia's little face. She cried and asked over and over why Mr. a'Coy would leave them, when her mama still needed help. And she thought since Mr. a'Coy was her friend, he wouldn't go off without saying goodbye.

Supper had been a sad affair. Rosemarie was amazed at how quickly they'd all grown accustomed to the presence of the friendly, helpful man. She also felt the loss of something else. An uneasy, unfamiliar feeling. She preferred not to name it. Or think about it much.

With a deep sigh she sat on the edge of the bed, and struggled out of her clothes and into her nightgown. After washing her face and cleaning her teeth with the supplies Chandler had put by her bedside, she crawled under the covers and attempted to sleep.

She lay flat on her back, her arms crossed over her middle. They'd get by. Every day her leg would continue to heal, and she would get stronger. The chickens were now cooped up again, thanks to Daniel, and the food in the root cellar would see them through the rest of the winter.

Most of all, the feelings Daniel evoked in her would end. No more would she sense the tingling when he accidently brushed against her, or the warmth of his hand on hers when he helped her from room to room. Hans had never inspired such sensations. But she must put those thoughts aside. Her children needed her. She was a woman grown, with responsibilities. Silly, girlish dreams and wishes were just that. Dreams.

The moonlight filtering through the window cast an eerie glow over the room. She shifted onto her side, clasping her hands together under her cheek. More than an hour passed before she felt herself drifting off.

Rosemarie's eyelid's popped open. What was that noise? In the scant moonlight everything in the room looked the same. Her heart sped up as she sensed someone else in the room. Knowing she was without male protection, had one of the soldiers come back to assault her? She rolled onto her back, her breath catching as Daniel walked through the bedroom door. He stopped just inside the room and stared at her. Slowly, he moved to her side and squatted down.

He studied her face, his eyes seeking an answer to a question she wasn't sure she wanted to hear. He ran his knuckles over her cheek. "I wanted to lead them away from here, so they would leave you in peace."

"I thought you were halfway to Kentucky by now," she whispered.

He smiled, flashing straight white teeth. "It crossed my mind, but you still need help."

"Is that the only reason you came back?" She inhaled sharply, amazed at what she'd asked him.

"No." He lowered his head, his breath fanning her face. "But I need to leave one day. You must know that."

"I do." The last words she murmured before he took possession of her mouth.

Daniel felt as if he'd come home. Home to the woman he wanted more than any other. He'd lied to her, and to himself, when he said he returned because she still needed help. *He* needed *her*. And he wanted her—in his bed and in his life. He groaned as he pulled her closer, and tilted her head to take the kiss deeper. He nudged her lips with his tongue, and she opened. The sweetness overwhelmed him. Soft, wet, like molten honey, he touched all the velvety parts of her mouth.

He moved away before he took it any further. If he didn't return to his bed in the barn right now, he never would. With the pull of the war tugging at him, he'd no right to make her his.

Daniel gazed into her passion filled eyes, a feeling of satisfaction washing over him. She would be his one day, of that he was sure. They'd passed a milestone this afternoon when she'd hidden him and then faced the Union soldiers. There was no going back.

"I'll see you in the morning." He whispered against her ear, and then tasted her sweet lips once more in a light kiss.

CHAPTER SIX

Early April, 1865

"I can't believe poor Hans is gone, and I wasn't here to comfort you." Susan McDonough clutched Rosemarie's hand, sorrow etched on her full face.

"I'm doing okay." Rosemarie attempted to pull her hand free from her neighbor's, who had descended on her with her husband, Jacob, and their four children.

Never too fond of Susan, who had a curiosity beyond polite, along with a well-developed propensity to gossip, Rosemarie had invited them into the house against her better judgment. Daniel was working in the barn, and the minute he appeared, Susan would pounce on him like a lion.

"Here Jacob and I hoped to ask Hans to help with our barn raising." She stopped as she reached the small table in the kitchen, surprise lighting her eyes. "Why, I'm sure you didn't even know the Rebels burned our barn down, now did you?"

"No, I didn't know that." Good manners required she offer them at least a cup of tea, when all she wanted to do was send them on their way. "Would you care for some tea? I have sweet biscuits left from breakfast."

Susan settled her large bottom into the kitchen chair, all set for a lengthy visit. "Why that would be wonderful, Rosemarie. It's been so long since we've talked."

You mean since you pried information out of me.

"Maybe while we're here, Jacob can do some chores for you. I'm sure you're havin' a hard time since Hans passed."

As usual, Jacob sat, not saying anything, letting his wife prattle on. It amazed Rosemarie how he put up with it.

"Mama, Mr. a'Coy sent me to fetch some water." Amelia rushed into the kitchen, one of Susan's girls following in her wake.

Susan turned to Rosemarie, her eyebrows raised. "Who?"

"Mr. McCoy. He, ah, is the hand I hired to help out for a while."

"Really?" Susan turned to Jacob and nudged him in the elbow. "You better go see this Mr. McCoy, make sure he's not a criminal."

"No." Rosemarie snapped. "Sorry." She turned to Jacob. "There's no need to trouble yourself, Jacob, he's been here for a while now, sleeping in the barn, and won't be much longer. He just needed some work, and then he'll be on his way."

Jacob glanced at his wife. One look at her glare and he rose. "No problem, Miz Wilson. It would be a good thing to take a look at the man." He slapped his hat on his head and left the house.

"Really, Rosemarie, how could you allow a strange man to stay in your barn? And with three children? Why, he could be a murderer. Or worse." She touched Rosemarie's hand to stop her from arranging biscuits on a blue and white flowered plate and leaned in close. "You know," she whispered, "I had a visit from some soldiers a while back who were looking for a very dangerous Rebel who escaped from prison!"

Rosemarie's heart thudded. Although no longer in a Confederate uniform, once Daniel opened his mouth, Jacob would know he was southern. She'd had another visit herself from Captain Nelson and his men, and got the distinct impression he knew Daniel was here. Luckily, Daniel had been away from the farm hunting, with the horse he'd stolen. The way things stood, he'd have to leave soon for his own safety.

Susan prattled on for well over an hour while Rosemarie kept her ear cocked, waiting for Jacob to rush in and announce that the Wilson farm harbored an escaped Confederate prisoner. No matter how much she strained, all she heard was the laughter and excited shouts of her children playing with the McDonough kids.

"Well, land sakes, I don't know where Jacob has gotten himself off too, but I have to get home and start my supper." Susan stood, shaking out her skirts. The two women walked to the front door, Rosemarie with visions of Jacob tied up in the barn and Daniel miles away. Even though she knew that day would arrive, and most likely very soon, the thought of him leaving caused a knot to settle low in her belly.

Ever since the night more than a week ago, when he'd returned and kissed her with a passion she'd never felt before, things between them had shifted. After his last kiss, he'd pulled away from her, ran his knuckles down her cheek, and left the room. The longing in her body kept her awake most of that night. She'd been embarrassed to admit to herself she wanted more. More of his kiss, more of his tender touch.

The next morning, she took extra pains with her hair, made sure she wore a clean apron. Then she laughed at herself. What was she doing? Daniel was an escaped Confederate soldier with a life to return to, if he wasn't re-captured first. She was a plain, work-worn, mother of three children. Obviously, nine years with Hans had left her aching for tenderness and caring. But this was not the man, nor the time, to imagine she'd found it.

But one glance at Daniel when he'd arrived at her bedroom door the next morning to help her into the kitchen wreaked havoc with her emotions. His warm smile and strong arms as he scooped her up and carried her down the hallway, had her heart thumping again.

More than once she'd caught hunger in his eyes, right before he shifted his gaze away. If it hadn't been for the distraction of the children, and the exhaustion of trying to work while her leg healed, she feared she would have done something foolish. Daniel was a hunted man, and it would serve her well to remember that.

No longer using the walking stick, Rosemarie hobbled to the front door. A sense of relief swept over her as Jacob and Daniel made their way from the barn to the house. She and Susan joined them as they reached the bottom of the porch steps.

"Seems like your man here has things under control," Jacob said as he slapped Daniel on the back. "The barn's clean, the wood's piled up, and it looks like he's gettin' your garden ready for plantin' in a few weeks."

"Where are you from?" Susan peered at Daniel, her eyes narrowed.

Jacob chuckled. "Won't do you no good to ask him questions, Susan. The man can't talk. He's been doing some kind of sign language thing with me, but I figured out what he was sayin'."

Rosemarie bit the inside of her cheek to keep from laughing.

Can't talk? Doing sign language?

"Well, I declare. I never met anyone who did the sign language thing." Susan turned to Rosemarie . "How do you manage to get him to work?"

Rosemarie kept her gaze from Daniel, knowing she'd burst out laughing if she looked at him. "It's not hard, actually, I just sort of point to things, and he knows what to do."

Daniel gave the woman a small salute, and turned toward the barn. Susan followed him with her eyes. "I don't know that I could be around someone who didn't talk."

"No worry, you would do enough talking for the both of you." Jacob turned and shouted for his children, who raced around the yard, chasing Missy, Amelia's barn cat.

"No, David, leave my kitty alone." Amelia ran after the ten-year-old boy, her arms outstretched.

Daniel stopped and squatted. The cat ran to him, and he gathered her to his chest. He glared at David as he handed the cat to Amelia and ruffled her hair.

"Well, your children certainly seem comfortable. Him being a stranger, and all. But I would be careful if I were you, Rosemarie. You just never know. You don't want to wake up one morning dead." Susan sniffed and headed to the wagon where four children scrambled up, pushing and shoving each other.

Within a few days, Rosemarie could hobble around well enough to do some chores. Daniel did quite a bit of hunting, skinned rabbits and deer, cut the larger animals into chunks, and stored them in the smokehouse.

With the help of the two younger children, Rosemarie managed to do laundry. Daniel set up the tubs for her in the mudroom, heated the water, and carried it. The children gathered all the dirty clothes while Rosemarie sat and washed and rinsed them. Then Daniel hung them on the clotheslines Hans had strung up years ago, joking with Chandler about how important it was for men to do women's work when they were needed. Somehow, she couldn't picture Hans doing laundry, no matter how far behind she got.

Daniel took Chandler hunting with him, and her son stood tall when they returned with two rabbits that he'd shot. "I told you I could take care of ya, Ma."

"Yes, I see that." She held back her laughter, enjoying the moment with Daniel as he smiled behind Chandler's back at the boy's pride.

Now that they had plenty of meat, supper was the time Rosemarie enjoyed the most. Once chores were done and Daniel and the children were washed up, they all hurried to the table, hankering for food.

The early spring sun dipped behind the barn, casting the yard and small house in dusky shadows. It had been another long day, but Rosemarie was happy with her accomplishments. Each day she grew stronger, and as thankful as she was for her health, the niggling thought in the back of her mind that Daniel would soon leave them, dampened her spirits.

"Can I help you finish up?" Daniel stood at her back, watching her ladle stew into a bowl. His nearness, and the smell of the soap he'd used to wash up, wafted over her. Her stomach did funny little jiggles every time he came near.

"If you want to pour milk for the children, that would help." She took a deep breath as he moved away. Rosemarie chided herself. This was crazy; she was an older, widowed mother of three. There was no place in her life for these feelings. Lt. McCoy had merely helped them over a rough spot, and soon he would be on his way.

Since when is he Lt. McCoy?

After placing the large bowl of stew in the center of the table, Rosemarie returned with the loaf of fresh baked bread and butter from the cold pantry. Daniel poured the milk for the children, and cold water from the pump for both adults.

As they all settled in, hands joined, heads bowed, they thanked the Lord for their food. As she took up her spoon, Rosemarie let her gaze roam over the group. Her children's faces were flushed from the cold air and outdoor play. They ate with enthusiasm, hanging onto

Daniel's every word. He discussed the fine art of whittling with Chandler, while Amelia peppered him with questions. Jace, his eyes heavy with fatigue, spooned the stew into his mouth.

Don't get used to this. Regardless of how he makes you feel, remember, this is all temporary. Daniel doesn't belong here.

As Daniel explained whittling to Chandler, he remained aware of Rosemarie across the table from him. Each time he'd glanced in her direction, she would shift her eyes, a slight flush on her cheeks. Could she possibly have the same feelings for him as he did for her?

Once recovered from the worst of her infection, the dark circles under her eyes disappeared and the sunken look to her cheeks filled out. She was truly a beautiful woman, even after years of hard work and bearing three children. Her full breasts, hidden under her work dresses and aprons, would fill his hands nicely. Earlier, as he watched her walk from the house to the barn, even with her slight limp, her hips swayed enticingly enough to cause him to re-adjust his trousers.

Her soft voice as she read to her children at bed time floated over him, bringing with it the sense of happiness and security he'd had as a child when his own mother did the same with him and Stephen. His gut twisted when he remembered the present time and place. He was a fugitive, in enemy territory, being hunted by soldiers.

They'd hidden the horse he'd stolen from the soldiers in the back of the barn, only letting him out to exercise, always concerned someone would ride up and ask questions. As much as he hated to admit it, the time grew near for him to leave.

"Mr. McCoy, when the weather gets warmer, will you take us fishing?" Chandler wiped his mouth with the back of his hand.

"Fishing." Jace nodded.

"Can I come, too?" Amelia asked.

Daniel pushed his plate away and leaned his forearms on the table. "I have to return to my regiment very soon."

"What's a regiment?" Chandler wrinkled his forehead.

"That's the group of soldiers I'm fighting the war with." Daniel glanced over at Rosemarie. She placed her spoon along her bowl and folded her hands in front of her.

Amelia left her chair and climbed onto Daniel's lap. "I don't want you to fight in a war." She stuck her fingers in her mouth, and rested her head on his chest.

His large hand smoothed her golden brown curls. "Sometimes we have to do things we don't want to do."

The little girl raised her soft blue eyes to him. "Like go to bed?"

He chuckled and hugged her. "Yes, like going to bed."

"Speaking of bed, it's time you all got washed up and in your nightshirts." Rosemarie stood and began collecting dishes.

Amid groans, the three children left the table and headed down the hallway.

"I love listening to you read stories each night." Daniel slid over on the settee to give Rosemarie room to sit.

"A habit my mama started when we were all young." She settled next to him. Very little pain radiated from her wound. In a day or so, she would be back to normal. And there would be no reason for Daniel to remain.

"Tell me about your family. Do you have siblings?"

Rosemarie smiled. "Oh yes. We were seven daughters and only three sons. Papa was not happy with all the girls." She turned toward him, her elbow leaning on the top of the settee, her head resting in her cupped hand. "In fact, he thought all those females were punishment from the Lord for something he'd done wrong in his youth."

Daniel grimaced. "That must have hurt."

She shrugged. "When you grow up with that attitude,

it doesn't seem as bad as it does to someone hearing it for the first time."

"Are you among the oldest, the youngest?"

"I was the last girl, one year older than the last boy, my brother Seth. Like the rest of my sisters, when I turned thirteen, Papa sent me out to work. I was lucky, though, to work for Mr. Oliver Morton, who's now Governor of Indiana. He's a real nice man."

"And how did you end up married to Hans Wilson?"

Even after all these years, her stomach still clenched when she remembered that day. "Papa came to the Judge's house when I was fifteen and told me he'd arranged for me to be married."

Daniel's brows rose. "Fifteen?"

Rosemarie nodded. "One year older than the sister before me."

Daniel blew out a low whistle.

"It wasn't so bad. I have three beautiful children."

"Yes, you do." Daniel moved closer and twirled a strand of hair that had fallen from her bun. "Makes sense, since they have a beautiful mother."

She studied his lips as he spoke, then raised her eyelids until her gaze met his. Her heart thundered at the hunger in his eyes. "I don't feel beautiful," she whispered.

"Oh, but you are." Daniel lowered his head, brushed his lips over hers. When she sucked in a quick breath, he pulled her closer and took possession of her mouth, probing her lips with his tongue. His palms skimmed over her curves, lightly at first, then with firmness, his fingers massaging her slim shoulders and her back muscles.

Rosemarie leaned into his hard body, her breasts crushed against his chest. Never before had she felt this heart-stopping desire. Her head spun, and her woman's core ached with need. To have him touch her, to feel his work roughened hand against her naked skin.

Daniel released her and loosened the buttons on her dress. She closed her eyes, felt the light touch of his feathery kisses on her eyelids, then her nose, her chin, and finally the soft, sensitive skin under her ear. He pushed the dress to her waist and slid the straps of her chemise off her shoulders.

His eyes darkened with passion as he skimmed her exposed skin, and then cupped her breast, kneading, pinching the nipple between his thumb and fore-finger.

Rosemarie threw her head back and moaned. He dipped his head, and pulled a pebbled nipple into his mouth. His teeth grazed the tip and then he suckled deeply, shooting waves of sensation to the apex of her thighs.

She glanced at his head against her chest, his mouth working her breast. She ran her fingers through his hair, pulling him closer, feeling the warmth and closeness.

"I want you, sweetheart." He raised his head, and caressed her cheek. "But I have no right."

Ever since he'd cut his hair and shaved his beard a couple of weeks ago, which revealed the strong chin with a cleft in the center, her hands had itched to run them over his face. Now she gave into the temptation and cupped his cheek. "I don't care."

"I have nothing to offer. I can't even stay to take care of you."

She closed her eyes, wanting him more than she'd ever wanted her husband. "I don't care. Just love me for tonight."

Daniel groaned and swept her into his arms. He strode down the hallway and pushed open the door to her bedroom, kicking it closed with his foot. He deposited her gently on the bed, his gaze never leaving hers as he pulled his shirt from his pants.

Rosemarie watched with fascination as he removed his clothes. For all the years she'd spent with Hans, she'd never seen him undressed. He'd always made sure the candles were extinguished before he crawled in alongside her.

But this man was worth looking at. His muscles rippled under golden skin covered with a light dusting of hair. He continued to stare at her as he reached for the buckle at his waist and unfastened his pants. Shoving them down, he stepped out of the trousers, kicking them free. He stood before her in all his male glory, taking her breath away. Her palms itched to caress all that golden skin, to tweak the hairs on his massive chest.

Her eyes roamed further down at his jutting manhood, eager and pulsing. Sitting up, she reached out her hand and touched him, amazed at the hardness underneath incredible softness. She'd never touched Hans in this way. Would his body have been as fascinating as Daniel's?

Not likely.

"Sweetheart, you're killing me here." He sat next to her on the bed, and within moments, after a few maneuvers, had her as naked as he was. His gaze roamed over her from her face to her toes, his eyes eating her up. "You are so beautiful, Rosemarie."

"No." She eased back, attempting to pull the sheet up to cover her body. "I've had three children. My body is no longer young."

"Ah, honey, your body is perfect. For me." He brushed the curls back from her forehead and slid her down, stretching out alongside her. "You are a woman who has borne children and nursed them from your breasts. It's what God intended when he made women as beautiful as they are. As beautiful as you are."

Tears sprang to her eyes at his words. No one had ever made her feel so happy to be a woman, for herself, not just as a body to provide relief for a man. Or a servant to see to his other needs. When she looked into his eyes she did feel beautiful. And desired. She cupped his cheek. "Thank you."

With a low groan from deep within, his large hand took her face and held it gently. His head descended and covered her lips in a slow drugging kiss. Thank God she was lying down, or she would surely have slid to the floor in a puddle.

She'd spent years being bedded by Hans, but had never been made love to until now. Daniel worshiped every part of her body, kissing, teasing, licking, until she was thrashing on the bed, begging him to finish what she ached for.

"Ah, sweetheart, I won't leave you wanting." He spread her legs apart and moved over her, resting on his forearms, cradling her face. He took his time easing into her, allowing for months without a husband.

Once he completely filled her, he burrowed his face where her neck and shoulder joined, whispering words of praise and of her beauty. He slowly began the ancient dance of lovers, moving in and out with a smooth motion. His body shifted to rub hers right where she needed to feel the pressure of his movements.

With as long as they'd been fighting the powerful attraction between them, it didn't take much time for her to splinter apart at the same time Daniel threw his head back and poured his seed into her.

He collapsed and rolled to the side, taking her with him. Reaching down, he drew the blanket over the two of them, tucking her securely against his side. Secure and cherished. That's how he made her feel.

She had no idea lovemaking could be so wonderful. Deep in her heart, she knew this was truly how the joining of a man and a woman should feel. As if she'd found her other half, as if she would never again be a complete person without Daniel.

He lazily ran his fingers up and down her arm. The sounds of her heart pounding and her lungs attempting to fill with air soon settled into a normal pattern as she drifted off to sleep in Daniel's arms.

CHAPTER SEVEN

Jolted awake by the sound of the bedroom door opening, Rosemarie's heart thumped as she gazed into the dim light. She was afraid it was one of the children, who would see Daniel lying alongside her. When the door fully opened, the man who occupied her thoughts stood there, completely dressed. She quickly darted a glance at the mattress, at the outline of where his body had lain. He moved further into the room, and sat on the bed next to her. One look at his face and she knew. He was leaving. Her stomach muscles clenched.

"You know." He took her hand in his. The warmth from his touch shot straight to her core. Tears rushed to her eyes and she blinked rapidly to regain her emotions. She'd known from the start he wouldn't be with them forever. But for the first time in her life she felt cared for, as though she meant more to someone than what she could do for them, or bring them.

She should be ashamed that she had given herself to Daniel, but in her heart she knew it had been right. At least she would have one night of glorious memories to sustain her throughout the coming lonely years.

"Yes," she whispered. "I know it's time."

He pushed the hair away from her forehead, leaned forward and kissed the spot he uncovered. "I wish I could stay." Daniel released her hand and stared out the window at the bare branches swaying in the late winter wind. "I wish there was no war, no north and south. No Union and Confederacy." His gaze met hers. "Most of all I wish I could stay here with you, love you every night, watch your belly swell with our child."

Rosemarie sat up and brought his hand to her cheek. "That's what I wish for as well." She dropped his hand and raised her chin. "But wishes are just that, Reb—wishes."

He smiled at the nickname she hadn't used in a while, then his lips tightened. "I hate that I'm not in a position to make promises."

"I know." Rosemarie clasped his large hand in hers. "The children will miss you."

"Only the children?" His heated gaze searched her face for an answer.

She slowly moved her head back and forth. "No."

In one swift movement, Daniel crushed her to his chest, claiming her mouth. Rosemarie parted her lips and he swept his tongue in. The intimacy of the act sent a shock wave through her body. She moaned and slid her palms upward, encircling his neck, pulling him closer.

Daniel raised his head and cupped her cheeks. "You are so beautiful. Inside and out." When her eyes filled again, he kissed each eyelid. Two tears tracked down her cheeks. He tucked her head against his chest and she inhaled deeply, trying to memorize his smell, and feel.

"When this war is over…"

"No." She pulled away. "Don't make promises." She stiffened her spine, and wiped the dampness on her face. "You have a whole different life, far away from us."

He took her cold hands in his warm ones. "No, sweetheart, I have no life far away from here. No life anywhere away from you. My family's land has been sold, my parents are both dead, and my brother, if he's still alive, is fighting with the Union Army."

Again he pulled her to him. "If I survive, I will return, even if I have to walk every step."

Rosemarie shook her head. "Don't say that. Please."

"Do you think I would make love to you and not plan a future if I were able?"

Unable to speak, she merely shook her head.

He sighed and set her away from him. "If I don't leave now, I never will. I'm still a wanted man." Daniel ran his knuckles across her cheek, stood, then made his way to the door.

"Where are you headed?" How could she make normal conversation at a time like this when her heart was breaking?

"To Kentucky. I'll be safer there. I'll try to hitch a ride to Virginia." He stared over her head, his jumbled thoughts visible on his face. "General Lee needs all the help he can get. Something tells me we're getting close to the end." He shook his head, as if to clear it. As his hand rested on the doorknob, he added, "I'm leaving the horse here for you."

Rosemarie swung her legs over the side of the bed and stood, wrapping her hands around her middle. "Take the horse. You have a long way to go."

"No. You need the animal here. I'll be fine. Get back into bed, it's cold."

"Daniel…"

He shook his head, and left the room, the soft click of the door closing like a dagger to her heart.

"Mama?" Chandler stood alongside Rosemarie's bed as she eased her eyes open, squinting at the sunlight streaming across the bed, bathing her face in warmth.

She'd spent the hours after Daniel's departure tossing and turning, her thoughts so jumbled, sleep remained elusive. She rose on one elbow, blinking away the grit from her aching eyes, confused at the amount of daylight. It must be way past the time they all generally awoke.

Rosemarie smiled at her son. "What time is it, Chandler?"

"I don't know, but Amelia and Jace are sick."

Rosemarie threw the quilt off, and stood. "Sick?"

He nodded his head. "Jace is crying that his throat hurts, and Amelia just threw up. I gave her the chamber pot."

They hurried to the children's room. Rosemarie pushed open the door and her stomach clenched. Her two younger children tossed in their beds, their faces flush with fever.

"Amelia?" She knelt beside her and smoothed back the hair from her brow.

Amelia stared back at her with glazed eyes. "Mama, I don't feel good."

The sound of Jace crying softly caught her attention, and she moved to his bed. The baby thrashed, his legs moving restlessly as he licked his dried lips. "Mama." He held his hand out, which Rosemarie took, alarmed at the heat radiating from it.

"Itchy," Amelia whimpered.

Rosemarie scooted back and lifted the child's nightgown. A rash covered her neck and chest. She checked Jace. The skin on his small body felt dry and scratchy, and he also had a similar rash.

"How do you feel, Chan?"

"My throat hurts a little, but I feel okay."

"I'll be right back." Rosemarie left the room, her heart racing. Childhood illnesses could kill.

Dust motes danced in the air as she hurried down the hallway to the parlor. In a few quick steps she reached the bookshelf Hans had built for her as a wedding present. Shaky fingers retrieved the worn copy of Gunn's Domestic Medicine, the well-used book her mother, Marie, had given her when Rosemarie was carrying Chandler. Rosemarie had memories of Mama leafing through the pages while a sick child or two writhed on their beds. Although her mother had managed to raise ten children, she'd given birth to fifteen. Two died at childbirth and the other three succumbed to childhood illnesses.

Brows furrowed, Rosemarie hastened to the bedroom, flipping the pages as she walked. She skimmed over symptoms of numerous diseases that struck children every year. Her eyes moved back and forth as she read the description under Childhood Diseases.

Symptoms of chicken pox include a rash on the patient's chest, then face. He will also complain of nausea, fever, headache, sore throat, and pain in both ears. As in all illnesses of childhood, chicken pox may be dangerous, and easily spreads from one person to another. The patient should be kept quiet, and indoors. If possible, a doctor should be consulted for instructions.

"Mama," Jace wailed right before he vomited onto the floor.

"Chandler, fetch me a pan of water and some cloths to cool your brother and sister down." She searched his face. "Are you sure you're all right?"

Chandler eyed the mess on the floor and swallowed a few times. "I think so."

She placed her hand on his forehead. No fever, so far.

"I want you to cool down Jace and Amelia while I clean the floor." From sheer habit, she headed to her bedroom to dress and fetch Daniel from the barn. She would need his help.

Then her thoughts stopped her as if she'd run into a wall.

Daniel was gone.

She was all alone with two, possibly three, children who could die. Tears welled in her eyes. Dear God, what could she do?

Rosemarie walked in circles, wringing her hands. Despite the clear US brand on the stolen horse's left shoulder, she needed to hitch it to the wagon and bring the three children into town to see the doctor. She would find a way to cover the marking.

"Mama, should I fetch Mr. McCoy, from the barn? He'll know what to do. " Chandler stood in the doorway to her bedroom.

"He's…" What? Gone forever. On his way back to the war. No longer able to help us. She sighed and sat on the edge of the bed. "Mr. McCoy left last night to re-join his regiment."

Chandler's face paled. Amazing that the Reb had been here just short of a month, and already her son had lost faith in her ability to handle things alone. She was their mother, she'd nursed them before.

But never all three at the same time, and with a serious illness.

"What will we do?" His voice quivered.

Rosemarie stared at him for a minute. "Go to the barn and hitch the horse to the wagon. We'll take Jace and Amelia into town to see the doctor."

Chandler raced away, and Rosemarie quickly removed her nightgown and pulled on a dress. Once the floor in the children's bedroom had been cleaned, she hurried outside with the feather mattress from the boys' bed and stuffed it into the back of the wagon.

The horse's US brand glared at her in disapproval. At the sound of retching, she turned to see Chandler emptying his stomach alongside the wagon. A sense of fear and urgency swept through her. "Go wash out your mouth, and then climb into the wagon and lie down."

"What about Jace and Amelia?" Chandler wiped his forehead with his sleeve.

"Don't worry, I'll get them."

Both children tossed on their beds, whimpering. She wrapped Jace in his blanket, and carried him outside. Back from his trek to the sink, Chandler reached for Jace and tucked him into the wagon bed. Once he was settled, Rosemarie rushed to the house and carried Amelia out.

"Mama, I'm so hot," her daughter whined.

"I know, honey. But you must keep the blanket

wrapped around you."

"Where we going?"

"I'm bringing you and your brothers to Dr. Kennedy in town. He'll know what to do to make you feel better."

"I like Dr. Kennedy," she whispered.

With everyone settled, Rosemarie threw another blanket over the horse to hide the brand, tied her bonnet strings with jerky movements, and then with a racing heart drove the wagon out of the yard.

A little over an hour later, Rosemarie urged the horse down the main street of Bartlett Creek, a small town standing not quite halfway between the Wilson farm and Indianapolis. With the three children sick, it had been a quiet drive. They'd stopped a few times to allow one child or another to lean over the side of the wagon and throw up.

The sun shone high overhead, but the air remained cool. Shops did a brisk business, with customers going in and out, carrying bags of goods. After a few minutes, Rosemarie noticed a sense of gaiety in the air. People greeted passers-by with smiles, men shook hands, and women hugged each other. Focused on getting her children to the doctor's house, she continued down the street, and turned the corner next to the saloon. The tinny jangle of a piano blared from the doorway, and from the sound of it, more than a couple of men had decided to drink their noon meal.

She pulled up in front of a white clapboard house. If she'd been able to ride into town when Hans had been shot, perhaps Dr. Kennedy might have saved his life. But left with no horses, she'd taken care of her husband herself. Guilt gripped her when she realized she would never have known Daniel, made love with him, if Hans had survived. Nine years of marriage to Hans had never moved her the way only a few weeks with Daniel had. Now he was gone, off to fight in the war, and she would most likely never see him again.

The door to the snug white and blue house opened before Rosemarie even knocked.

"What brings you all the way out here, Mrs. Wilson?" The doctor's wife, a round-cheeked woman of middle years, wiped her hands on her apron and smiled at Rosemarie.

"My children are sick. Is the doctor in?"

"Not at the moment, but he should be back very soon." Mrs. Kennedy stepped onto the porch, and patted Rosemarie's arm. "Let's get the little ones into the house."

The two of them hurried down the porch steps. Chandler was able to walk, and Mrs. Kennedy and Rosemarie carried the younger ones.

"We'll need to cool them down while we wait for the doctor." Rosemarie laid Amelia on a small cot in the doctor's infirmary. "Can you get me some cool water and a cloth?"

"Certainly, dear. I'll be right back."

Rosemarie tugged at the ribbons of her bonnet and laid it on the table next to Jace. A quick check of foreheads revealed all three children burned with fever.

"Here we are." Mrs. Kennedy swept through the doorway with a pan of water and several cloths.

Rosemarie wet one of the rags, and ran it over Jace's legs, arms, and face. Mrs. Kennedy did the same with Amelia.

"I think they may have chicken pox." Rosemarie could taste the fear in her mouth as she wrung out the cloth and moved to Chandler's bed.

"Now, dear, don't you fret. I had two of my boys come down with chicken pox and they got through it just fine."

Rosemarie sat back on her heels and regarded the woman. "Really?" Taking a deep breath, she returned to her chore, somewhat reassured.

"Yes. When Dr. Kennedy returns, he'll take a look at

them and see what needs to be done."

As Rosemarie tended to her children, her thoughts wandered to Daniel, on his way to Virginia. The beauty of their love making the night before brought tears to her eyes. She couldn't help thinking the experience was unique. She'd never felt anything near that with Hans. When Daniel had entered her, slowly, afraid to hurt her even though she'd born three children, her heart filled. His tenderness, so different from her past experience with men, made her want to grab onto him, never let him go. Then within hours he'd kissed her goodbye and left.

About fifteen minutes later, the front door of the house opened, and soon the doctor filled the doorway to the infirmary. "What have we here?"

"All three of my children are sick. I think it may be chicken pox."

Dr. Kennedy set his hat on the counter next to Chandler's cot and rested his medicine bag alongside it. After shrugging out of his coat, he knelt next to Chandler and pulled up his shirt. He ran his hand over the small bumps running from his chest to his neck. Then the doctor scooted over to Amelia, and then Jace, repeating the process with each one.

"Looks like you're right, Mrs. Wilson. All three have chicken pox."

She bit her lip. "Is it dangerous?"

The doctor rubbed his chin. "It can be. But most times it's not. What we need to do is get them into bath water with oats in it."

"Oats?"

He chuckled. "Yes. I've learned that helps to ease the itching, which they'll be doing plenty of soon." He rolled up his sleeves and continued. "If we make it a cool bath, it will also help bring down the fever."

Rosemarie took a deep breath for the first time since she had awoken that morning.

"How is Hans?" the doctor questioned over his

shoulder, as he washed his hands at the sink.

"Hans died from a bullet wound a few months ago."

Dr. Kennedy studied her as he dried his hands. "Tell me about it."

Rosemarie stood and shook out her skirts. "Confederate soldiers came to our farm back in November. They took everything that wasn't nailed down, and when Hans tried to stop them from taking our last horse, one of the soldiers shot him."

The doctor shook his head. "Damn the war."

"Yes." She hugged her middle. "He didn't die right away. I nursed him for a couple of days, but the infection took him."

Mrs. Kennedy reached out and squeezed Rosemarie's arm. "I'm so sorry, dear. How have you been managing by yourself?"

"It's all right. We're getting along."

"I know you don't want to hear this, but you should think about marrying again. I know it hasn't been long, but you can't take care of three children and a farm by yourself."

The only man I would consider marrying is off to fight a war. On the other side.

"Well, at least you don't have to worry about soldiers raiding your homestead anymore."

"Yes. There isn't anything left for them to take."

The doctor stared at her for a moment. "I'm talking about the war being over."

Rosemarie's stomach dropped to her feet. "What do you mean?"

"Why, General Lee surrendered to General Grant just yesterday."

All the breath left her body, as she reached behind her and sat on the edge of Chandler's cot. "The war is over?"

"Yes, indeed. Jed at the newspaper office got a telegram late last night. The news is all over town. Now we can get back to normal living again, and stop killing all our young men."

Daniel. He's on his way back to Virginia. And the war is over.

She had to find him. Being on the road, he wouldn't know about the surrender. Her heart leapt. They could be together! In the short time since he'd left, it would only take her a few hours racing with the horse to find him. Her head spun with the possibilities.

"Mrs. Kennedy." She turned to the woman, who viewed her with furrowed brows.

"Do you think it's possible for me to leave my children with you? Just for maybe a few hours, or possibly a day?"

"I guess that would be all right. What's the matter, dear? You turned so pale all of a sudden."

Rosemarie stood and licked her dry lips. "I have to find someone. A man." She hurried on when the woman's eyes widened. "He was helping me at the farm for the last few weeks. He's, well, he's from the south, and he was headed back there."

"Oh, my." Mrs. Kennedy breathed out.

"You said my children's illness isn't serious?" Her heart pounded so hard, the other two people in the room must have heard it.

"Chicken pox can be serious, but I don't see any evidence that your three won't do just fine, as long as things progress as I expect them to. We can do the baths, cool them down, and for the most part, just watch over them and feed them plenty of liquids."

Rosemarie twisted her hands, and turned again to Mrs. Kennedy. "Would it be a burden to you? I really don't want to impose."

Apparently having recovered from Rosemarie's announcement, the doctor's wife smiled with a twinkle in her eye. "You go on ahead and chase down your man, Mrs. Wilson." She chuckled. "I guess my advice to you on remarrying came a bit late."

"I'm not so sure of that, but I need to try."

Mrs. Kennedy made a shooing movement. "Go on. Do what you need to do. We'll take care of these young 'uns."

Rosemarie snatched her bonnet from the counter and hugged the woman. "Thank you so much. If all goes well, I should be back by tomorrow at the latest."

"Mama?" Amelia called to her from the bed.

"Yes, honey."

"Are you going to get Mr. a'Coy?"

"I hope to find him. Will you be all right here with Dr. and Mrs. Kennedy?"

"Yes. Please tell Mr. a'Coy we want him to come back to take us fishing."

Rosemarie bent and kissed Amelia on the forehead. She spent a few minutes saying goodbye to the two boys, and then left.

The main part of town was still in a celebratory state. Now she understood the townspeople's actions earlier. The best plan would be to leave the wagon at the livery and go after Daniel on the horse. She pulled up to the stable and jumped down.

"Can you take care of my wagon for a day or so?" She spoke over her shoulder to Jedediah, the livery owner, as she unharnessed the horse. "I'll also need to borrow a saddle from you."

"Sure thing, Mrs. Wilson." He walked closer and ran his thumbs up and down his suspenders. "Did ya hear about the surrender?"

"Yes I did. I'm grateful it's all over."

She smiled in his direction, then waited while he fastened the straps on the saddle.

"Thank you so much." She swung up onto the horse and headed toward the main street.

Things had gotten quite a bit livelier since she'd entered town earlier. A red, white and blue banner with the words "The War Is Ended!" hung from two buildings, stretched across the street. Small flags and signs appeared in store windows. The noise and music in the saloon had grown louder, and it appeared school had been let out early because a dozen or more children ran up and down the street with barking dogs following along.

Rosemarie grinned and headed south, where she would take the road Daniel had planned to use.

Please God, don't make him have changed his mind.

As she reached the end of town, a group of Union soldiers headed toward her. She recognized the man in front as Captain Nelson. Four soldiers rode behind him, with the last soldier riding double. As she grew closer, the sight of the second man, his head hanging down, hands tied behind his back, caught her eye, making her breath catch. The shirt and pants he wore had hung on the hook by her back door for months.

Her heart thumped as she recognized Daniel. She kicked the horse and rode up to the group. "Daniel!"

Daniel's head snapped up and his eyes met hers.

"Captain, why is Lt. McCoy tied up?"

The captain smirked. "How is it you know my prisoner, ma'am? And by name? And rank?"

Realizing her mistake, she stiffened. Then remembered the war was over. He couldn't do anything to her now. "You need to release him. The war is over."

Captain Nelson stretched his lips in the imitation of a smile. "Well ma'am, it seems I can't do that."

"Why not?"

"First of all, since my men and I have been on the road for a couple of weeks, I haven't gotten official word that the war is over. So after Lt. McCoy here spends a night in the town jail, I'll be taking him back to Camp Morton in the morning."

Rosemarie furrowed her brows. "But then you'll release him?"

"Afraid not, ma'am."

She shook her head in confusion. "I don't understand."

Daniel looked her square in the eye as Captain Nelson spoke.

"Well, see ma'am, Lt. McCoy will be hung for stealing Federal property. In fact"—he leaned forward—"for the horse you're riding right now."

CHAPTER EIGHT

Daniel's lips tightened as Captain Nelson's words hung in the air. Rosemarie had gone so pale he was afraid she'd pass out and tumble from the horse. Still stunned to have run into her in town, he nevertheless ate her up with his eyes.

Leaving her last night had been the hardest thing he'd ever done. Even surviving and escaping prison camp had not torn him up that way. Rosemarie was everything he ever wanted in a wife and lover. He loved her children, could be very happy working her farm, but most of all he desired her. This strong, beautiful, passionate woman was the one he wanted to spend the rest of his life with. But it appeared that his life would soon be cut short.

"Captain, may I speak with Lt. McCoy?" Rosemarie had recovered some of her color, and now her eyes flashed in anger as she stiffened and made her request.

"Afraid not, Mrs. Wilson. We're headed to the jail right now. My men and I are anxious to get baths, a meal, and a little fun before we return to the fort tomorrow. If you want to talk to the sheriff about seeing your lover, here, that's up to you."

"Shut your filthy mouth!" Daniel felt the heat rise to

his face, and his fists clenched behind his back.

"I suggest you keep quiet, prisoner. You ain't in no position to demand anything." Captain Nelson turned and tipped his hat at Rosemarie. "Ma'am." Then he moved his horse forward, the other men following. After a few steps, he turned. "Oh, and we'll be taking that horse back now, as well, ma'am."

"You can't leave her here without a horse," Daniel growled.

"Soldier, you don't seem to understand that you have no say." He smiled in Rosemarie's direction. "Remove yourself from the horse, Mrs. Wilson."

Rosemarie slid off the animal and began to unfasten the straps. "This saddle belongs to the livery," she snapped.

"Fine. We'll be by your place soon to pick up the saddle that was on the horse when your lover stole it."

A surge of anger so strong raced through Daniel that he broke the piece of leather fastened around his hands. He jumped from the horse and pulled Captain Nelson from his. Taken completely by surprise, Nelson received three good punches before he recovered himself and yelled to his men. Two soldiers grabbed Daniel by his arms. Nelson rotated his neck, dusted his jacket, and pulled on the cuffs. "Hold him."

"No!" Rosemarie screamed as the captain pulled back and slammed his fist into Daniel's face. Blood spurted from his nose. Nelson drew back and drove his fist into Daniel's stomach several times. When he sagged toward the ground, Nelson kicked him in the ribs.

"Get him up and drag him to the jail."

Rosemarie ran to Daniel, but one of the soldiers grabbed her arm. "Ma'am, it's best if you go about your business. Like Captain Nelson said, if you want to visit him in the jail later, go see the sheriff."

With one soldier on either side of him, Daniel was dragged to the sheriff's office and pushed through the door. Captain Nelson already stood in the center of the room, rubbing his jaw which had already started to bruise.

"This the man you been searching for?" The sheriff stood and snagged a ring of keys from the wall.

"Right. Military prisoner." Captain Nelson glanced in Daniel's direction, a smirk on his face. "He'll be hung in the morning, once we get him back to Camp Morton. My men and I will be at the hotel overnight."

The sheriff led Daniel and the soldiers down the short hallway and opened a cell door. One of the soldiers placed his palm against Daniel's back, and shoved. He landed on his knees, next to a small cot. No one spoke as the sound of the cell door locking resonated in the air.

Rosemarie watched the two soldiers haul Daniel away. Suddenly sick to her stomach, she clutched her middle, and eased herself down onto the saddle alongside the road. Daniel was to be hung for stealing the horse.

Her heart thudded and she pushed away the hair blowing into her eyes with a cold, shaky hand. She had to do something. The first thing was to get Dr. Kennedy to take a look at Daniel in the jailhouse. After the beating Captain Nelson had given him, Daniel would need medical attention.

Leaving the saddle where it sat, Rosemarie hurried back into town. After a short visit with Jedediah, he agreed to collect the saddle she'd left behind. The next stop was the doctor's house.

"Back already? That was quick," Mrs. Kennedy said, her smile faltering as she took in Rosemarie's appearance. "What's the matter, dear? You look upset."

"I need Dr. Kennedy to take a look at someone in the jail. He's been beaten, and I doubt the sheriff would send for your husband because the prisoner is a military detainee."

"Come in, let me get the doctor."

Rosemarie followed Mrs. Kennedy down the hallway

and entered the infirmary. All three children were fast asleep.

"How are they doing?"

"Just fine. The doctor and I bathed them in the oat water, and he gave them a little something to help them sleep. Only Amelia still has a fever, but it's slight." She patted Rosemarie's hand. "Let me tell the doctor you're here."

Rosemarie sat on a chair next to Jace's bed, where the boy peacefully slept. The rash had spread to his face and arms. Thank goodness they were in the care of the doctor. Even though chicken pox was one of the lesser evils in childhood diseases, it eased her mind to have them here when she needed to focus on Daniel.

"Now tell me about your young man." Mrs. Kennedy bustled into the room. "The doctor will be right down."

Rosemarie paced, wringing her hands. "Daniel is a confederate soldier, recently escaped from Fort Morton military prison." She cast an uneasy glance at Mrs. Kennedy. When the woman's expression didn't change, she continued. "He came to our farm looking for a place to bed down for the night. I had a serious cut on my leg." She stopped her pacing and looked the woman in the eye. "He saved my life. The cut had become infected." After taking a deep breath, she went on. "Then, he stayed for a while, helping with the chores, teaching Chandler how to hunt, making scrambled eggs for Amelia because she hates oatmeal …"

Unable to continue, she pushed her fist into her mouth, holding back tears. The image of Daniel swinging from a rope overwhelmed her.

"What's this about someone needing attention at the jailhouse?" Dr. Kennedy entered the room, rolling down his shirt sleeves.

"He's a friend of Mrs. Wilson's," Mrs. Kennedy answered, giving Rosemarie time to compose herself.

"Can you come with me to the Sheriff's office?"

Rosemarie's voice was thick with emotion.

"Let's go." The doctor picked up his bag and they left the house.

The streets of Bartlett Creek continued to display flags, banners and a general sense of celebration. Dr. Kennedy and Rosemarie remained oblivious as they hurried to the jailhouse. She couldn't help but think how happy she would have been with the war coming to an end, if it had not been for Daniel being captured.

No longer would she need to cringe at the sound of horses riding up to her farm house, afraid one army or another would take more from her family. She could plant all the corn she wanted and not worry about losing it to military provisions. But none of it would matter if Daniel wasn't with her.

Dr. Kennedy held the door for her as they entered.

Sheriff Jake Morris swung his feet off the desk, bringing his chair upright. He shoved a small book into his desk drawer. "What can I do for you, Doc?"

Despite the circumstances, Rosemarie smiled at the sheriff. A large man, he'd been hired by the town five years ago, when the former sheriff retired. With very little crime to deal with, Jake spent a lot of time reading penny novels, which he thought was a deep secret. The entire town knew of his private habit, but out of respect, and a genuine liking for the man, no one mentioned it to him.

"I understand you're holding a man here who needs some medical attention."

"You talking about that Reb in the back?"

The doctor nodded and headed toward the cell. "Can you open the door, please, Jake?"

The sheriff threw Rosemarie a curious glance, then grabbed the keys and followed the doctor. She was right behind him.

Daniel sat on the small cot, his eyes closed, and his head resting against the wall. Both of his eyes were swollen, and dried blood crusted his split lip. Rosemarie drew in a sharp breath, which caused him to open his eyes. "I don't want you here."

"Daniel, please."

"Sheriff, please escort Mrs. Wilson from the jail."

"No, Daniel," she cried as the sheriff took her by the arm.

Daniel winced as he stood and walked to the bars of the cell. "Rosemarie, this is no place for you. Please, do me a favor and forget me."

She yanked her arm from the Sheriff's hold. "No. I will not forget you, Daniel McCoy. Neither will Amelia, Jace, and Chandler. We want you back with us."

He slowly shook his head. "I will be hanged as soon as I'm returned to Camp Morton. Captain Nelson will not budge. Please go to your children." He turned his back and shook his head at the doctor when he attempted to look at his injuries. "Leave me be. There's no point in medical treatment for a dead man."

"You might be willing to give up, Daniel. But I'm not." Rosemarie continued to speak to his back. "Don't give up. Please."

"Ma'am," the sheriff said softly. "It appears my prisoner doesn't want you here, and I have to agree that the jailhouse is no place for a lady."

Rosemarie pulled herself up to her full height and addressed Daniel. "I'll be back. Just as soon as I figure out what to do."

When no answer was forthcoming, she turned toward the sheriff. "All right. I'm leaving."

He tipped his hat and led her to the front door.

The sound of the sheriff's door closing behind her echoed in her ears as she stood on the boardwalk. What to do now? She held herself tightly, as if to keep her entire person from unraveling like a ball of yarn. If Daniel was to be saved, she needed to get herself under control.

"Mrs. Wilson, can I offer you a ride somewhere?" Dr.

Kennedy walked up behind her, his face softened with compassion.

She shook her head and swiped at the tears gathering in her eyes.

Dr. Kennedy took her by the arm. "Come. Mrs. Kennedy will make us some tea, and you can visit with your children."

Any other time, Rosemarie would have appreciated the aroma of fresh baked bread and simmering stew from the pot on the stove in Mrs. Kennedy's kitchen. As it was, it took all her willpower not to run to the privy and empty her stomach.

"Dear, I believe Mrs. Wilson could use a good, strong cup of tea." The doctor pulled out a chair for Rosemarie and indicated she should sit.

Mrs. Kennedy glanced at Rosemarie and tsked. "Oh, my. Yes, let's have some tea. Then maybe you could eat a little bit of supper with us."

"Thank you, I appreciate your kindness." Rosemarie slumped in her chair, then abruptly stood. "I need to see to my children."

"They're all sleeping, nice and peaceful-like."

Rosemarie smiled at the woman. "Thank you so much for all your help. I'll just take a peek at them."

Her eyes filled again at the sight of her three children, all asleep, faces dotted with red marks. Although it had never seemed likely, given their differences and the war, Daniel would have made a wonderful father to them. He had so much patience with all their questions and requests.

She moved into the room and smoothed back the curls from Amelia's face. How grateful the little girl had been for having scrambled eggs instead of oatmeal. And Chandler. She gently touched his cheek. So proud to be hunting, providing food for the family, as Daniel had explained was his duty. Soon her little boy would be turning into a young man. He would need the guidance of a strong, capable man to help him along that path.

Jace whimpered and she hurried to his side.

"Thirsty."

Rosemarie eased his head up and encouraged him to drink from the cool glass of water Mrs. Kennedy had left on the table alongside his cot. Like his brother and sister, he no longer burned with fever.

"How do you feel, honey?" She settled him in and smoothed the colorful patchwork quilt.

"Sleepy," Jace mumbled as he rolled over and closed his eyes.

"Sleep is the best thing for them." Dr. Kennedy entered, his confident presence filling the room. "Your tea is ready."

Rosemarie stood and smoothed her skirts. While dealing with her children, she'd forgotten about Daniel for a minute. But it all came rushing back as she followed the doctor down the hallway to the kitchen. Mrs. Kennedy had set the table with tea things, and bowls of stew and fresh bread.

Although her stomach had previously roiled at the thought of food, Rosemarie suddenly realized she hadn't eaten anything since supper the night before. Maybe a little bit of food would restore her and help her come up with a plan to save Daniel.

The first few bites of the fragrant stew brought her hunger back full force. The three of them chatted amiably while they consumed the stew and made good use of the bread. Leaning back in her chair, Rosemarie took a sip of the tea, a full stomach relaxing her for the first time that day.

"Mrs. Wilson, if you're going to help Lt. McCoy, you're going to have to come up with a plan."

Rosemarie closed her eyes and nodded at the doctor. "I know, and I've been wracking my brains trying to think of something." She sat forward, her hands in her lap. "The only thing I can think of is going to Camp Morton in the morning and pleading with the Fort Commander."

Dr. Kennedy shook his head. "Colonel Ambrose Stevens is in charge of Camp Morton, and I've heard the man is out of the state right now. It seems he was called to Washington."

Rosemarie drained her tea cup and turned to Mrs. Kennedy. "I would like to attempt a visit to the jailhouse again. But first I'd like to feed my children, if that is acceptable to you."

"Of course, dear. I think something light on their stomachs would go well." She spoke to Dr. Kennedy. "How about a bit of beef broth for the young ones?"

"That's an excellent suggestion. It will build up their strength and not tax their systems."

After spending time spooning broth into their mouths, Rosemarie read them a few stories, and soon all three children were nodding off. She tucked them in, kissed each one on the forehead, and headed to the hallway. Dr. and Mrs. Kennedy sat in the parlor, she with her knitting while the doctor read the newspaper.

Despite the twinges of fear in her stomach, Rosemarie enjoyed the peacefulness of the Kennedy parlor. A fireplace glowed, with enough heat to warm the room. The doctor and his wife had been married many years, and raised four boys, who now were off, living their own lives. The companionship the couple presented brought a hitch to Rosemarie's heart. She and Daniel could have this. Would they be together like this many years from now, or would she forever mourn what never was?

"The children are all settled down and off to sleep." Rosemarie swallowed against the thickness in her throat.

Mrs. Kennedy put down her knitting and regarded her. "Please return after your visit to the jail. The doctor and I would love for you to spend the night here with us."

"You are very kind," Rosemarie said.

"If you stop by the kitchen before you leave, I wrapped a package for Lt. McCoy."

"Thank you so much." She gathered the tea towel with bread, cheese and fruit inside, and left the house.

The celebration of the war's end continued, the saloon seeming to be the focal point of the festivities. Rosemarie pulled the borrowed shawl from Mrs. Kennedy tight around her body and hurried past the revelers, covering the distance from the doctor's house to the jail quickly. From half a block away, the building that housed Daniel appeared dark and quiet. Her breathing hitched. Had Captain Nelson changed his mind and traveled to the Camp tonight instead of in the morning? She ran the last few steps and pulled on the Sheriff's door. Locked.

Completely panicked now, she pounded on the door and was greeted with silence. Her mouth went dry. "Daniel!"

The only sound continued to be the shouting and laughter from the saloon. Rosemarie moved around the building until she spotted a small window with bars. "Daniel?"

"Who's there?"

She slumped with relief at the sound of his voice. "It's Rosemarie. I've brought you some food."

"Wait a moment. I'll drag this cot over so I can see you."

After a few minutes, Daniel's face appeared in the window, bathed in moonlight. "Honey, you shouldn't be here. The town's in an uproar tonight because of the war ending. I don't think it's safe for you to be on the streets. And I told you it's useless. You should be with the children."

"*And I told you* this afternoon, Lt. Daniel McCoy, I'm not giving up. And the children are fine. Well, almost fine. They all have chicken pox."

"What?" He gripped the bars on the window. "Where are they? Who's with them?"

She smiled. "Calm down. They're all three at Dr.

Kennedy's house. They're doing fine, Mrs. Kennedy tells me. The doctor doesn't anticipate any problems with them."

Daniel dragged his hand down his face. "Thank God."

"I've brought you some food. Have they fed you?"

He shook his head. "I think the sheriff is too busy keeping the peace over at the saloon to worry about feeding a man who's to be hung in the morning."

"Stop saying that!" The panic in her voice surprised her. "We will get you out."

"Darlin', you need to face this. Captain Nelson is personally anxious to see me swing. He's a man who doesn't like to be made a fool of, and escaping from his prison, and then stealing one of his horses right from under his nose doesn't sit well."

"Here, take this." Rosemarie shoved the wrapped food between the bars, her hand shaking.

"Maybe you should have brought a saw." He chuckled.

Her eyes grew wide. "Can we do that?"

"No, Rosemarie." He set the package down and gripped the bars again. "Don't involve yourself in anything like that. You have three children to think about."

Her eyes filled with tears, and Daniel reached through the bars, clasping her hand. "Please don't come here again. It kills me to see you and not be able to touch you, to hold you. I love you, and want so much to make you my wife, to help raise your children, and be there when you birth ours." He swallowed a few times. "But it's not meant to be. You must leave now, see to your children, and forget our time together."

"Never." She crossed her arms under her breasts and shook her head. "I'll never forget our time together. I love you, too, and refuse to believe we won't be together again."

Daniel smiled briefly. "Go now. I want to remember

you this way, standing in the moonlight, your beautiful face looking up at me."

"Daniel, please..."

He jumped from the cot, disappearing from the window, and, she feared, from her life.

CHAPTER NINE

Daniel pushed aside the package of food, and lay on the cot, his mind numb with pain. The thought of hanging in the morning was not a pleasant one, but seeing Rosemarie and the suffering in her eyes, overshadowed even his impending death. How he ached to hold her, comfort her. Everything he'd ever wanted in a lifetime partner and lover, stood outside that window, a mere few feet from him. But she might as well have been on the other side of the world.

"Good night, Daniel. I love you." Her soft voice drifted through the window before her light footsteps moved away, leaving him choking on the silence.

He sat up and hung his head, hands dangling between his bent knees. Even if he managed to escape, the only place he'd be safe was far away from Rosemarie. He could grab her and the three children and run, but with no land, or a way to earn a living, he'd be condemning them all to starvation.

Heavy-hearted, Rosemarie left the jailhouse and continued on to Dr. Kennedy's house. When Hans had succumbed to his injury back in November, she'd felt a

94

kind of numbness, and a sense of abandonment. But certainly not this overwhelming feeling of loss, of having left part of herself behind. Panic raced through her. She had to find a way to avoid this disaster. After years of coldness from her father, and then Hans, she'd finally found a man who made her feel wanted and loved.

"Evenin' Mrs. Wilson." The sheriff tugged on the brim of his hat as he approached her. He stopped and placed his hands on his hips. "Things are gettin' a little bit boisterous tonight, what with everyone celebratin' the end of the war. I don't like you out walkin' by yourself. Where ya headed?"

"I'm staying with Dr. Kennedy and his wife. It's just a few blocks."

"No matter, ma'am. I'll walk along with you. Make sure you get where you're headed with no problems."

They continued on, the early spring night air pleasant against her face. "Sheriff, can you do anything to help Lt. McCoy? Anything at all?"

"Ma'am, I'm real sorry about your trouble, but seeing as how he's a military man, and the charges against him are from the Union army, there's not a heck of a lot I can do."

She sighed and wrapped her arms around her middle. "Is there anything you suggest I do?"

"Maybe if you went to Camp Morton and talked to the commander?"

"No." She turned to him. "He's been called to Washington. Right now Captain Nelson is in charge."

Jake shook his head. "I don't know what else to say. You need someone higher up than Nelson." He took his hat off, ran his fingers through his hair, and tugged it back on. "Captain Nelson sure seems to have it in for McCoy. Almost like it's personal."

"It is." She winced. "Lt. McCoy came to my farm after escaping from Camp Morton. I was suffering with an injury that would have killed me if it weren't for his arrival right then. He saved my life.

"Then he stayed to help with the chores until I recovered. One day Captain Nelson and a few of his men arrived at my farm. They were searching for Lt. McCoy. The Captain got a bit antagonistic in his questioning, so Lt. McCoy left the hiding place I sent him to and stole one of Captain Nelson's horses to distract him."

The sheriff let out with a low whistle. "That must've made him mad."

"Oh, yes."

They arrived at the doctor's house, and the sheriff turned to her. "I sure wish I could help you. The little bit of contact I've had with the Lieutenant convinces me he's a good man. But there isn't anything I can do."

"I understand. Thank you for seeing me home."

"My pleasure, ma'am." He tugged on the brim of his hat and turned to head back to town, crossing over the street in the direction of the saloon, where the noise had grown.

Rosemarie climbed the few stairs, and was greeted by Mrs. Kennedy, who had opened the door as if she'd watched for her.

"How is Lt. McCoy?"

"Reconciled to his fate."

The doctor's wife patted Rosemarie's arm. "Come into the parlor with the doctor and me. Maybe if we put our heads together, we can think of something."

The last thing Rosemarie wanted was to sit in the parlor and watch the doctor and his wife eye her with pity.

"I'll take a look at my children first."

"Fine, dear. You do that, and then join us."

Jace's fever had risen a bit, but Chandler and Amelia slept on peacefully. After requesting a pan of cool water, Rosemarie bathed Jace until the little boy settled down again. Mrs. Kennedy had made a paste that she'd put on the children's pox marks which seemed to sooth them. After applying the mixture once again to Jace, she kissed all three children on the forehead and returned to the parlor.

Dr. Kennedy folded his newspaper and laid it aside. "Mrs. Kennedy tells me your young man is not feeling hopeful."

Rosemarie shook her head and settled on the settee alongside the doctor. "Afraid not. And I'm terrified the morning will come before I think of something to help."

Her gaze shifted to the newspaper resting on the cushion. She scanned the headline. Governor Morton had issued a statement praising the Union Army and hoping for a quick re-joining of the Confederate states. She picked up the paper and began to read. The governor had given a speech in front of the Capitol building in Indianapolis. She smiled. Her former boss loved giving speeches.

We are happy to see the conflict come to an end. With my fellow Americans, I mourn the loss of so many brave men who gave their lives to keep the country intact. I also mourn the deaths of the brave men who fought with the Confederacy, believing their cause to be noble and right...

She skimmed the article, reading further down where the reporter added his own comments.

Although the Governor backed President Lincoln's war measures, he had always denounced excessive military arrests, resisted the draft, and freeing Southern slaves until the president issued his emancipation proclamation on January 1, 1863...

Rosemarie's heart banged against her chest and her mouth dried up. Governor Oliver Morton, the man she worked for years ago. The man who attempted to talk her father out of marrying her off at such a young age. Who'd taught her to read and write. He had been her champion then, and could be now.

She burst from the settee as if shot from a cannon. Mrs. Kennedy's head snapped up and she grabbed her throat. "What is it, dear?"

"Governor Morton!"

"What about the governor?" Dr. Kennedy regarded her with wide eyes.

"He…he." She swallowed several times. "He can help me."

The doctor rose and gently pushed Rosemarie back onto the settee. "You've become quite pale, Mrs. Wilson, you need to calm down." He eased her head between her knees and patted her back. "Take a deep breath, and then tell us what you mean."

"I'm fine" she batted his hand away and stood again. "I worked for the governor when I was a young girl. I lived at his home, and he was always fond of me, treated me like a daughter in some ways. When my father arrived to tell me about my arranged marriage, Governor Morton gave him a tongue lashing."

She bent and picked up the newspaper. "It says here that Governor Morton has always been against excessive military arrests."

Rosemarie turned to them, both members of her audience staring at her with slack jaws. "Don't you see? He might be able to stop Daniel from hanging."

"But, the hanging is tomorrow, and the governor is in Indianapolis, a three hour ride from here," the doctor protested.

"I don't care. I have to try. This is my only chance, don't you see?" She used her index finger to wipe tears from her eyes.

Mrs. Kennedy stood and embraced her. "Of course we understand, dear. Were I in your place, I'd do the same for Dr. Kennedy."

"Thank you," Rosemarie whispered.

"Well, if you're making that trip in time to help Lt. McCoy, you need to get ready to go." Dr. Kennedy stood and patted her on the shoulder. "You may use our horse, Mellow. That would be faster than a buggy."

"Yes, faster." Her words came out breathless.

"I'll fix you a small meal to take with you." Mrs. Kennedy quickly left the room.

Dr. Kennedy frowned. "I don't like the idea of you

riding alone that distance."

"I'll be fine. It's a straight road, and hardly anyone travels it at night."

"That's precisely my problem with it." He gave her a curt nod. "I'll lend you my pistol to take with you." He also hurried from the room, leaving Rosemarie pacing and wringing her hands.

This has to work.

She checked the cherry wood grandfather clock, taking up the entire corner of the Kennedy's parlor. Fifteen minutes past eleven. If all went as she planned, she'd arrive at the governor's mansion in the middle of the night. Should she wait? Leave closer to dawn? If only she knew what time Captain Nelson planned on departing in the morning.

No, she couldn't take the chance. Even if she had to wake the governor from his bed.

Mrs. Kennedy bustled into the room. "Here, take this food with you, and my heavier jacket, it will keep you warm."

Footsteps coming down the stairs caused both women to turn as Dr. Kennedy entered, waving a pistol.

"Doctor, for heaven's sake, what are you doing?" Mrs. Kennedy screeched.

"This is for Mrs. Wilson to bring with her."

"Oh, my goodness." She patted her chest. "You scared me half to death!"

The road from Bartlett's Creek to Indianapolis was, as expected, completely deserted. Most likely a vast amount of the citizenry were celebrating. The earth under the horse's hooves allowed her to go at a quick pace. As a well-traveled road, it provided a solid ride.

Rosemarie shifted in the saddle and pulled the collar of the borrowed jacket up to cover her ears. The night air was chilly, and she thanked God for the Kennedys' generosity.

Moonlight cast long shadows over snug little farmhouses and sizeable barns as she continued on her journey. The odor of fresh dirt from furrows of freshly plowed fields rose to her nostrils, the familiar smell comforting her. Silence was her only company, broken only by the heavy breathing from her and Mellow as she maintained a brisk pace.

Her thoughts drifted to Daniel. For the first time since she'd met Captain Nelson and his men on the road in town, hope filled her heart. Hope that she would have the man who had captured her heart and her children's devotion. Memories of their time together before he left raised her temperature. She'd never imagined the joining of a man and a woman could be so wonderful. The only recompense she'd ever gotten from her intimacy with Hans were her three beautiful children.

Now that the initial excitement for her plan had worn off, fatigue engulfed her. Her backside hurt from the constant jarring of the horse. She shifted in the saddle, but no matter how she moved, after about ten or fifteen minutes, she was sore again. Maybe if she nibbled on the food Mrs. Kennedy had packed for her, it would help to keep her awake.

Munching on a juicy red apple, Rosemarie bent low over the horse and galloped on toward Indianapolis, praying the horse wouldn't lose his footing in the dark.

Rosemarie banged on the Governor's door for the third time. The inky black sky, with thousands of stars lighting it, confirmed it was still a few hours before dawn. She held her breath and rested her ear against the large wooden door. Yes. That was the sound of footsteps approaching. Someone fiddled with the lock and then the door opened. "Yes, miss?"

The servant had apparently been roused from his slumber. Rosemarie pushed the guilt aside. "Mrs. Rosemarie Wilson to see the Governor."

White hair stood in tufts from his head as the servant regarded her, his eyebrows rising. "Madam, it is barely a few minutes past three o'clock in the morning."

She nodded. "Yes. I know. May I come in and wait for him, please?"

He opened his mouth, then closed it, repeating the action until he resembled a fish. "The governor won't be receiving guests for several hours."

Rosemarie ran her sweaty palms down the front of her dress. "Look, Mr...." When he didn't answer, she continued. "It is a matter of life and death that I speak with the governor as quickly as possible."

When he moved to close the door, she slapped her hand against it. "Please. Please, sir, just let me wait inside until dawn. Then I really must insist you wake Governor Morton so I may speak with him."

"Madam," his voice rose, "kindly remove your hand from the door, or I shall summon the police."

"What the devil's going on down there, Billings? I'm surprised you haven't woken the entire neighborhood." Governor Morton hurried down the stairs, tying the belt of his silk dressing gown.

"I'm so sorry, Governor, but this woman insists on entering and waiting to speak with you."

"For heaven's sake, madam," the governor pulled the door open. "You don't knock on people's doors..." He stopped, his eyes wide. "Is that you, Rosemarie?"

"Yes. It is me, and I need help. Right away." With the door opened further, she edged her way into the entranceway.

"Of course, of course, come in. Please."

The servant, suddenly seeming to notice his appearance, smoothed his hair and brushed the front of his red and white striped sleep shirt.

"Billings, show..." he glanced in Rosemarie's direction.

"Mrs. Wilson," Rosemarie added.

"Mrs. Wilson to the parlor. I will join her shortly."

The servant bowed. "Yes sir." He turned to Rosemarie. "Right this way, madam." He conducted her to the parlor with all the dignity of a man dressed in the finest livery to be had in Indianapolis. Rosemarie covered her mouth with her hand to control the giggles as she followed him, his pale, hairy legs leading the way.

Three quarters of an hour later, Governor Morton entered the parlor, dressed as if it were two o'clock in the afternoon. He strode in his familiar manner, crossing the room in a few steps. "It's so good to see you, Rosemarie." He grinned as he took the seat across from her. "I just wish it were a bit later in the day."

"I'm sorry to have arrived at such an hour, but I need a favor, and it was important I come right away."

They both turned as Billings knocked lightly on the door and pushed in a cart filled with coffee, tea, biscuits, jam, and fruit.

"Ah, here we are." The governor turned to Rosemarie. "I thought whatever you needed to discuss would go down much better with some food."

Tears flooded her eyes at the familiarity of this home, this man. He'd been like a second father to her in the years she worked for him. A smidgen of guilt nudged at her with the realization that she'd not visited him since the day she left. Her eyes had filled with tears that day too, as he hugged her goodbye and she left with her meager belongings to a new life she'd had no say in.

Not that the years with Hans had been horrible. He'd never struck her, and provided well for her and their children. If there was no softness in the man, he at least didn't make demands on her that she wasn't comfortable with. She gave herself a mental shake. This reminiscing wasn't solving her present problem.

The governor sipped from his coffee cup and leaned back, a look of pleasure on his face. "So what is this problem that brings you to my doorstep in the middle of the night?"

Rosemarie told her story, starting with Hans' death, the months of fear and loneliness, and then Daniel's arrival and all that evolved since then. When she finished, crumbs from the biscuit she'd worried into bits covered her lap.

Governor Morton was silent for a few moments after she finished, then he stood, shoving his hands into his pockets. "I've been against the brutality of this war." He turned to her. "On both sides." He stared into the distance and continued. "This war will go down in the history books as the worst conflict this great country of ours ever had." He began to pace, lost in his thoughts. "Every single soldier who bled to death on the field was an American. Every limb cut from a screaming soldier belonged to one of us. We killed our own brothers, uncles, sons, and fathers. Battle fields in both the north and south are saturated with the blood of our young men. How shall we survive as a nation with so many of our promising youths dead or wounded?"

Rosemarie licked her dry lips. Time was passing, and she needed his help. The sky had lightened since she'd begun her story.

"I'm sorry, my dear. I realize you're probably anxious to save your young man, and here I am rambling on as if I stood before an audience at a rally." He grinned and took his seat. "Tell me what you want me to do."

"I need someone with authority to stop Lt. McCoy's hanging. The Commander at the camp has been called to Washington. You are the only person above Captain Nelson who can stop this."

He gave her a curt nod. "Excuse me." The governor rose and walked to the door, shouting for Billings. The servant appeared within seconds.

"I want you to take a note to the Western Union office right away." He moved to a small desk in the corner and pulled out a piece of paper with the Governor's Seal on top. Dipping his pen into the inkwell, he began to write.

Rosemarie took in a deep breath. Hopefully, the missive would reach the camp before Captain Nelson followed through with his plans. Then an idea formed that made her heart twist. She didn't trust Captain Nelson. She chewed her lip as Billings left the room, the note in his hand.

"May I ask one more favor?" Rosemarie stood, her fingers clenched.

Governor Morton leaned back in his chair. "What else?"

"I have reason to believe Captain Nelson is taking this entire thing personally. I fear he may ignore the telegram."

The governor frowned. "Surely he wouldn't ignore a direct order from the Governor?"

"No, probably not. But, who's to know when the telegram will arrive? Even if it's later found he disregarded your instructions, it will be too late to save Lt. McCoy."

He nodded and pulled another piece of paper from his desk drawer, and wrote again. "Here. I suggest you ride to Camp Morton with this in your hand."

"Thank you so much. I will never forget your kindness."

A slight flush rose on the governor's face, and he waved her away. "Just go save your young man. That's all the thanks I want."

She bent and kissed him on the cheek.

"And don't wait another nine years to visit again."

With the paper in her hand, she left the house.

CHAPTER TEN

Daniel must have dozed off, as he was jarred awake by the sound of the cell door swinging open. "Got some breakfast here for ya, Lieutenant." The sheriff held a small basket that he placed on the edge of the cot. "Haven't seen hide or hair of Captain Nelson, so I thought I'd better feed ya. No telling how long they caroused last night."

Rubbing his palms over his face, Daniel stood. "Thanks, sheriff. I appreciate it."

"Sure seems ya got yourself in a lick of trouble."

Daniel nodded. "Can I get some water? I'd like to clean up a bit."

The sheriff swung the cell door closed and headed out toward the back. He returned a short while later with a pan of water and a small square of cloth. He slid them under the bars. "I'll clean everything out when you're gone."

When you're gone.

Today was most likely the last morning he would wake up. His eyes shifted to the small window where he'd touched Rosemarie's hand last night, while he cursed the wall that separated them. Now the moonlight had disappeared, leaving the buildings across the street glowing in the orange haze of sunrise. How soon would the captain come for him? Would they hang him the minute they hit the fort, or give him time to contemplate his fate?

The water in the pan was cold, but it felt good on the injuries his face had taken yesterday. After cleaning his face and teeth, Daniel ran his wet fingers through his hair. He shoved the pan into a corner and pulled the basket to him. Two warm biscuits, jam, and a small jar of coffee. He unscrewed the lid and drank the hot, bracing liquid. Although they smelled wonderful, his stomach rebelled at the thought of eating the biscuits.

Once he finished the coffee, Daniel stretched out on his cot, his hands behind his head. The ceiling above him was cracked, the paint chipped. His gaze roamed the room, the stark walls, small cot, slop bucket in the corner, and the bars on the cell door. Keeping him in, away from those he loved.

Before long his thoughts drifted to exactly where he didn't want them to go. Rosemarie. The woman he'd intended to return to when the war was over. To marry her, love her, help raise her children. A slight smile hitched his lips.

Amelia with her hatred of oatmeal, the appreciation in her bright eyes when he'd made her scrambled eggs. The pride in Chandler as he held up a rabbit he'd shot the last time they hunted. And little Jace, giggling as his arms raised, wanting Daniel to put him on his shoulders. How he would have loved to see them all grow into adulthood.

The sound of footsteps and deep voices pulled him from his musing. Captain Nelson and two of his men stood outside his cell. The sheriff arrived right behind them, the ring of keys in his hand.

"Time to go, southern boy." Captain Nelson sneered. "You ready to swing?"

Daniel muttered a curse under his breath and stood. He wouldn't give Nelson the satisfaction of showing the fear that tightened his belly. "Anytime, Yankee."

Captain Nelson scowled and nudged the sheriff. "Get the bastard out of there. We've wasted enough time as it is."

Once again Daniel's hands were tied behind his back. They escorted him down the hallway and outside to the bright sunlight. Two other men and six horses gathered in front of the jailhouse. Across the street, several shopkeepers stopped sweeping and gossiping, and stared.

"How do you expect me to mount the horse with my hands tied?"

Nelson gestured to one of the soldiers standing next to him. The young man, not yet out of his teen years, quickly untied the leather strap. Daniel mounted the horse. "Don't see as how I can ride either, with my hands tied up."

"No matter, dead man. One of my men will have a gun pointed at your back the entire ride. Either swing from the rope or get shot in the back, makes no difference to me."

Captain Nelson and his men all straddled their horses, and with a wave of his hand, Nelson moved them forward. Daniel was positioned between the captain and two young soldiers in the front, and the rest behind. The click of a gun by a soldier to his rear reinforced the captain's threat.

The two hour ride to the camp passed quickly. As they rode through the main gate, Captain Nelson led the men to a different location than the one Daniel had escaped from several weeks back. "Danforth," Nelson directed his comments to the soldier alongside him, "lock the prisoner up. I'm going to the office to get the paperwork done for his hanging."

The level of activity in the camp had increased since Daniel's departure. News of the surrender of General Lee had apparently reached the men. Already groups of men, ragged and weary, rode into the fort in creaking wagons from the fighting fields.

Danforth nudged Daniel with his gun and indicated

he should dismount. Daniel slid from the horse, and with a soldier on either side, entered a small room. A desk with papers scattered about sat in the middle of the space, with several chairs in various positions. A large map hung on a wall between two windows.

"In there." The young soldier motioned.

Daniel walked the short distance to one of four cells in a room behind the office. After being locked in, he sat on the cot and leaned against the wall, awaiting his fate.

Captain Nelson entered his quarters and laid his sword and gun on his desk. A rap on the door caught his attention. "Enter."

A middle aged soldier, with a belly that hung over his belt, saluted as he move into the room. "This telegram just came for you, Captain."

"Thank you, soldier." After nodding at the man, Nelson opened the paper and read, his eyes moving over the words. His jaw worked, and he felt his face flush.

"Goddammit!" He crumpled the paper, then fisted his hands on his hips, staring out the window. After a few minutes, he tore the missive into small pieces and tossed them into the fireplace.

"Time to go, Reb." Captain Nelson smirked at him from the other side of the bars.

After the door unlocked, Daniel stepped out, and the soldier standing next to Nelson tied Daniel's hands behind his back.

"Don't I get to see a preacher?"

"No. We don't have one here. You'll have to ask the good Lord to forgive your black soul all by yourself. Get moving."

As he stepped from the building, Daniel blinked at the bright sunlight, his eyes riveted on the platform with the noose hanging from it. This was it.

I'm so sorry, Rosemarie. Please don't mourn me for too long.

Take care of Chandler, Jace, and Amelia. Hug them for me and hold them close.

Daniel climbed the steps and walked to the center. The young soldier standing guard positioned him, and then slid the rope around his neck.

"Have any last words, soldier?" Captain Nelson stood, arms crossed.

"Stop!"

All three men glanced toward a woman, her skirts above her knees, hair flying in the breeze as she rode a horse right up to the platform, yanked on the reins and slid to the ground.

Rosemarie?

She looked magnificent. All the righteousness of an avenging angel radiated from her. Her hair tumbled down her back, her face was flushed. She gasped to catch her breath, her chest rising and falling. With her hands fisted at her side, and eyes flashing, she marched up to Captain Nelson, drew her arm back, and punched him square in the jaw.

Oh my God. Now we'll both hang.

The soldier on the platform jumped down and grabbed Rosemarie, wrenching her hands behind her back.

"Leave her alone," Daniel shouted. Turning to the other soldier on the platform with him, he growled, "Cut me loose."

Confused with the turn of events, and eyes bulging at the attack on the Captain, by a woman, no less, the soldier withdrew his sword and cut the ties binding Daniel's hands together. After yanking the rope from his neck, Daniel ran down the steps.

"You dirty, stinking bastard!" Rosemarie attempted to free herself, but the soldier held tight. "Governor Morton sent you a telegram this morning, telling you to halt this hanging."

The captain rubbed his chin. "I received no such information."

"Strange. I was right there in his parlor three hours ago when he sent his man with the note to the Western Union office."

"I have no idea what you're talking about. Proceed with the hanging." Nelson glared at the soldier. "Who authorized you to free his hands?" The captain's face contorted in anger.

"No you don't." Rosemarie yanked herself free from the befuddled soldier. "I have another note right here, signed at the same time by Governor Morton." She shoved the paper into his hand. "You can all see for yourself this is the Governor's seal on that paper. If you hang Lt. McCoy, I'll make sure you're thrown into prison for the rest of your miserable life.

"That is if they don't hang you for disobeying a direct order from the Governor of Indiana." Her eyes swept the area, the other soldiers staring wide-eyed, their jaws slack. "And I have witnesses."

Daniel moved to her, placing his arm around her shoulders, pulling her close. They both stared at the captain.

Captain Nelson opened the paper with jerky movements. A deep flush rose from his collar to his hairline. He crushed the paper in his hand and glared at her before tossing it to the ground. His jaw worked, the vein in his neck pulsing. "Release the prisoner."

He turned and strode away, the ball of the wadded up paper that saved Daniel's life bouncing in the breeze behind him.

Daniel placed his hands on Rosemarie's shoulders and turned her toward him. "I love you. You are the most beautiful woman I have ever laid eyes on."

She sagged with relief and smiled at him, her eyes twinkling. "I bet you say that to all the women who save you from a hanging."

"No, sweetheart. Only one." He lowered his head and took possession of her mouth. Something he intended to do every day for the rest of his life.

CHAPTER ELEVEN

With them riding double on Mellow, it took Rosemarie and Daniel a few hours to arrive at Dr. Kennedy's house. Both of them fatigued from the morning's events, they had ridden in silence, Rosemarie in front of Daniel, his arms wrapped securely around her.

"I must admit when I awoke this morning, I never thought to see this town again." Daniel gazed around as they came to a halt. He slid off Mellow's back and reached up for Rosemarie. Once she was in his arms, he gave her a light peck on the tip of her nose. "That's all for now. Once we get back to the farm, I'll give you a proper kiss."

He took a deep breath, filling his lungs with warm spring air. No more hiding, he was a free man. Free from the Confederate army and free from the clutches of Captain Nelson. Frankly, he didn't know if the governor had the authority to have him released, but with the man's backing, and the war over, the chances of anything coming to pass when the fort commander returned was slight.

Hand-in-hand they strolled up the doctor's steps and banged the knocker. A pleasant woman who must have been the doctor's wife opened the door, her expression of concern immediately turning into a bright smile. "Mrs.

Wilson. I see you saved your young man."

"Indeed I did, Mrs. Kennedy." She grasped Daniel's arm. "This is Lt. Daniel McCoy, formerly a Confederate soldier."

"Ma'am," he nodded.

Mrs. Kennedy stepped back and swept her arm out. "Please, come in. I see the doctor will have to attend to your injuries."

"How are my children?" Rosemarie asked as she followed Mrs. Kennedy down the hallway.

"They've been awake for a while. All three ate a bit of breakfast, and their fevers are gone."

"Praise the Lord," she murmured.

"Mama!" All three children shouted at once.

"And Mr. a'Coy," Amelia added. "You found him, Mama!"

Chandler stared at him. "What happened to your face?"

With everything else that had occurred, he'd forgotten about the beating he'd taken yesterday. "I ran into a bit of trouble, son, but Dr. Kennedy will fix me right up."

"Can we go fishin'?" Amelia asked.

Daniel sat on the edge of her cot and pulled her onto his lap. "Yes, we sure can, Miss Amelia. But first you and your brothers have to get better."

"Will you have to go back to your regiment again?" Chandler's eyes held the fear of a young boy who had shouldered too much already in his young life.

"No, I sure don't. The war is over."

"Who won?"

"I'm afraid no one, son. Both sides lost a great deal. But the Confederacy is the one that surrendered, and we are all one union again."

"Is that good?" Amelia said before tucking her fingers into her mouth.

"Yes, angel, that is very good, although I'm afraid a

lot of people won't think so for a long time to come. Hopefully we'll all heal eventually."

"Speaking of healing, I heard your young man has agreed to some doctoring after all." Dr. Kennedy entered the room, a huge grin on his face.

Daniel stood and shook the doctor's hand. "Thank you for helping my family."

Dr. Kennedy's grin grew wider. "Your family? I guess we're going to be looking at a wedding sometime soon."

"Well, seeing as how I haven't even had a chance to ask the lady for her hand, I can't rightly say. But in any event, it was *my* family you took care of."

"Mama, are you and Mr. a'Coy going to get married?" Amelia asked.

Rosemarie cast a glance in Daniel's direction. "Well, no one has asked me."

Daniel grabbed her hand and dragged her from the room. "We'll be right back," he flung over his shoulder as he hurried her through the doorway.

Once they were in the front parlor, he tugged her to him and wrapped his arms around her. "Mrs. Wilson, I love you with my entire being. I want you by my side for the rest of our lives. I want to raise Chandler, Amelia and Jace. And whatever children the good Lord blesses us with.

"Will you say yes to my plans, and make this wonderful day even better?"

Her eyes flooded with tears. "Yes, Reb. I will say yes to your plans since they are very much like my own."

"God, I love you," he murmured before his mouth covered hers in a searing kiss.

Since they had to wait for Daniel's black eyes to go back to normal, and for the children to recover from the chicken pox, it was a few weeks before the morning of Rosemarie's wedding arrived.

She arose to the scent of late spring flowers drifting

through the open window. Tonight she and Daniel would join together right here in this bed as man and wife. Always conscious of her reputation, Daniel had rented a room in town that he paid for by cleaning the saloon after it closed each night.

Every day, however, he spent with her and the children. He planted corn, helped Rosemarie start her vegetable garden, and began repairs on the barn that would soon house the wild horses he planned on capturing to begin his horse farm.

His soon-to-be wife thought the idea was a wonderful one.

A knock sounded on her front door and she hurried to allow a few women from the church to enter. They had arrived to help her dress, and to set up for the small reception they would have when they returned from speaking their vows.

The sounds of feminine chatter and excitement followed them as they took over her kitchen, placing warm dishes at the back of her stove, and the cold ones in her ice-box.

"Now it's time to get the bride dressed," Abigail Wetherby announced as she wiped her hands on a dish cloth and smiled brightly.

"Mama, can I help you dress, too?" Amelia looked up at her, eyes wide with anticipation.

"Of course, you can, sweetheart. And you have your new dress to wear, too."

The little girl jumped up and down and clapped her hands. "And what about Jace and Chandler?"

"I don't think they will be as excited as you are to dress in their best clothes for a wedding, but we'll make sure they look just fine when we leave for the church."

Daniel ran his finger around the inside of his collar and cast a weak smile at Reverend Potter. "I wonder what's taking them so long."

The preacher placed his large hand on Daniel's shoulder and squeezed. "We still have a few minutes until the service. They'll be here."

As the last word left the preacher's mouth the door at the back of the church opened and a crowd of women entered. In the center of the group stood his bride. His chest swelled with love.

Her light blue dress trimmed with lace fit her curves perfectly. As she turned to speak to Amelia, he got a glimpse of her hair that had been arranged in some sort of a bun at the back of her neck. Blue flowers circled the bun, the same flowers that she held in her hand.

Rosemarie bent to Chandler and spoke to him. He took Amelia and Jace's hands and walked to the front of the church, helping them into the pew and getting them settled.

Mrs. Dickinson at the organ began playing, and Rosemarie took the few steps from the back of the church to where he stood. He reached out and grasped her hand, "You look beautiful."

She smiled at him, and his insides turned to mush. This brave, wonderful woman would soon be his. They turned to face the preacher who would bless their union before God and man.

Several hours later, the twenty or so guests departed the farmhouse with hugs and well-wishes. The ladies had served the food and cleaned everything up, insisting Rosemarie take her wedding day off.

Daniel stood on the front porch with his arm wrapped around his wife, his children darting all over the yard, playing with Amelia's cat. As he turned her to head into the house, all his thoughts were on their bedroom and the pleasures that awaited them once the children were settled for the night.

"Mama, look. Here comes another visitor." Chandler pointed in the direction of the road leading up to the farmhouse.

Rosemarie raised her hand to her forehead to block the setting sun. A man walked the path, the fatigue in his body evident by his halting steps. He stopped for a moment, seeming to take in a deep breath, then continued on his way.

"Daniel?" Rosemarie said as her new husband stared down the road, his eyes growing wide. "Is something wrong?"

He shook his head and slowly descended the steps. As he continued toward the traveler, his heart sped up and his guts twisted. Once he was sure his eyes weren't playing tricks on him, he picked up his steps until he was practically running toward the man.

"Daniel?"

"Oh, my God. Stephen? I was afraid you were dead."

The younger man collapsed into Daniel's arms. "Not quite, big brother, not quite."

The End

Did you like this story? Please consider leaving a review on either Goodreads or the place where you bought it. Long or short, your review will help other readers discover new authors and make purchasing decisions!

Please turn the page for an excerpt from *Stephen's Bride*, Daniel's brother's story.

When Stephen McCoy leaves the Indiana farm he shares with his brother Daniel, Daniel's wife Rosemarie, and their four children to go into town to load up on supplies, he never expects to return with a bride.

Indiana, May 1867 —Calliope Bender arrives in town and steps off the stagecoach in a wedding gown, carrying a wilted bouquet. She is running from an unwanted marriage but still in need of a husband — one who will agree to a marriage of convenience. Eager to build a home for himself, Stephen agrees to Calliope's conditions, despite the fact that the idea of a "marriage in name only" doesn't sit well with him. Neither one of them is looking for love, but will it creep up on them when they aren't looking?

STEPHEN'S BRIDE

Chapter One

May, 1867
Indiana

Stephen McCoy tightened the final strap on the wagon hitch, and happy with his work, headed to the white clapboard farmhouse. He pushed open the front door and strode to the kitchen. Rosemarie McCoy, his sister-in-law, sat at the kitchen table shoving mashed potatoes into his niece, Lucy's eleven-month old mouth.

"I'm ready to go. Do you have your list ready?"

She nodded at a piece of paper on the table. "Right there."

He picked up the list and looked it over. "All right, I'm headed out, then." He touched Lucy on the tip of her nose, the baby smiling at him as mashed potatoes ran down her chin. "Where's Daniel?"

"He's trying to tame that new stallion he bought last week. I swear he won't be happy until he breaks his fool neck." She stood and dropped the bowl of potatoes and the spoon into the sink. Then grabbing a cloth she ran it under the water spout and proceeded to clean up the baby.

Stephen watched her efficient movements as she tended to her baby and prepared to put her down for her nap. Once again he felt like the fifth wheel on a wagon. She and his brother had made a good life for themselves after the War Between the States had ended. Rosemarie's three children, Chandler, Amelia and Jace, along with the addition of their daughter, Lucy completed their family.

Daniel worked hard on the farm Rosemarie had been left by her late husband, and Daniel had managed to put away enough money to start his own horse farm. Although Stephen was more than grateful for Daniel and Rosemarie taking him in when he'd returned from the War sick, wounded, and exhausted, the last few months he'd had the urge to have something of his own.

He knew exactly what that something was, too. He wanted his own horse farm. He and Daniel had been raised on a horse farm in Kentucky, which their mother had been forced to sell during the war to pay the taxes. Now Daniel was settled with a beautiful wife, four wonderful children, a thriving farm, and the beginnings of a horse farm.

Stephen's dream, one he'd been saving for ever since he was able to rise from his sick bed and join Daniel two years ago. Every single penny he didn't need he tucked away, along with money he'd picked up by doing odd jobs in town.

He slipped the list of supplies he was to get in town and headed for the door. Rosemarie stood with Lucy on her hip, ready to put the baby down for her nap. "Don't forget to pick up Chandler and Amelia from school before you return home."

"Have I ever forgotten my niece and nephew?" he asked as he opened the door.

"Yes," his smart-aleck sister-in-law with a fantastic memory said.

"Once." He grinned at her and the baby and left the

house. Four year old Jace ran toward him from the barn where his papa was working the horses. "Can I go with you, Uncle Stephen?"

He ruffled the boy's fine brown hair. "Sorry, partner. Not this time. After I get all the supplies your mama is wanting into the wagon, along with your brother and sister, there won't be room." He squatted and viewed the boy. "Next time, okay, partner?"

Damn. He shouldn't have done that. The bullet he'd taken on a bloody field during the War still rested near his hip. The surgeon at the time said it wasn't worth taking out, and now he suffered pain in that spot and had to be careful about getting on his knees.

At the glum expression on Jace's face, Stephen leaned in close. "How about I bring you a licorice stick?"

The boy's eyes lit up, and he nodded furiously. "Yes. I like licorice sticks."

Stephen rose to his feet with a groan and climbed onto the wagon bench. "You stay here and take care of your mama while your papa is working with the horses, okay?"

"Yes, sir." The little boy actually saluted which had Stephen grinning. He snapped the reins at the horses and started toward town.

The hour ride in the old wagon was taken up by him talking nonsense to the horses and pondering his life. He'd met a couple of women at church and church picnics, but no one took his interest. He'd like to have a family and a place of his own someday, but he still wasn't sure he wanted to put his heart at risk.

The letter he'd received from Jenny Foster when he was recovering from his bullet wound had hurt more than getting shot. Although she'd promised to wait for him, she wrote that she was not getting any younger, and the war seemed to be dragging on forever. Consequently, she had accepted a proposal from Martin Devin, a store owner in their home town and had married the man before she'd even sent him the letter.

No, he would like to marry and settle down, but he wouldn't marry someone he had fallen in love with. Once was enough for him. Maybe he could find a nice spinster, or war widow and marry to give her his name and financial support. She, in turn, would help with the chores and provide him with children.

He sighed and ran his fingers through his hair. And offer her what? Room in his bed in his brother's house? He really needed to make some plans. With four children, Daniel could certainly use the bedroom Stephen now occupied.

The road became smoother as the town came into view. Bartlett Creek had been passed over and forgotten during the war, but now that so many Confederate soldiers were returning to empty plantations and burned out cities in the south, they headed north, and the sleepy little town had grown quite a bit.

Not necessarily in a good way, either. Vagabonds, derelicts, and flat out criminals had taken up residence in the southern part of town, making areas of the once safe and comfortable town almost as dangerous as the bigger cities.

The wagon rolled to a stop in front of the General Store. Stephen climbed out and headed into the store.

"Good morning, Stephen. Come for supplies?" Mae McFadden, owner of Bartlett Creek General Store greeted him as she dusted items on the shelves with a feather duster. A clean white apron covered her bulk. "Mr. McFadden will be down in a minute to help you with loading when you're ready."

Stephen pulled the list from his pocket and placed it on the counter. "Be sure to throw in some licorice sticks for the little ones."

"Is that darling little Lucy ready to have one, too?" She grinned at him as she perused the piece of paper.

"Nah. I'm afraid not. If Rosie caught me sneaking

one of them to the baby she'd have my head."

"She'd also have your head if she heard you call her 'Rosie.'"

He winked at the store owner. "Let's keep that our little secret, eh? I like to call her that when she's mad at me."

"Now what would she ever have to be mad at you about? You have to be the easiest going fella I've met in a long time."

"I think I'm too much like my brother."

"She loves your brother." Holding the list, Mrs. McFadden began to pull items off the shelves. She turned to him, two tins of tea in her hand. "You need a wife of your own, Mr. McCoy."

He placed his hand over his heart. "Now why would you say that, when my heart belongs to you?"

"Go on with you. Not only am I married to Himself, but I'm old enough to be your grandmother."

He grabbed a licorice stick and bit down on it, harder than he meant to. A wife. A place of his own. A family. All the things his older brother had. Would they always be just out of his reach?

"I have my great-niece, Barbara Sue coming to visit me at the end of the month. She just buried her husband." Mrs. McFadden eyed him speculatively. "She needs some cheering up."

Great, just call on Stephen McCoy, the cheerer up of recent widows. "I'll keep that in mind." He shoved the rest of the licorice into his mouth and headed for the door. "I need to see Hans about the wheel I left with him to repair the last time I was in town. I'll be back in a bit."

"No hurry," she waved at him. "It will take me some time to get this all together. Leave your wagon and Mr. McFadden can load it up for you."

The heels of his boots tapped a cadence as he strode down the boardwalk. He doffed his hat to several women who walked along, shopping bags dangling from their arms, some with little ones hugging their skirts. He stopped briefly to allow the afternoon stagecoach to pass in front of him before he crossed the street to the smithy.

After conducting his business there, he returned to the boardwalk just in time to hear a sweet voice. "May I have your attention, please?"

Stephen stared across the street and grinned. A young woman dressed in a wedding gown, holding a bouquet of wilted flowers had climbed onto the roof of the stagecoach and shouted from the top of her lungs. "I need someone to marry me."

***

Calliope Bender took a deep breath and licked her dry lips. Waving her bouquet, she looked around at the few people who had gathered around her. "Is there a man here who is willing to marry me?"

This had been such a bad idea, but the only one she could come up with to save herself, and her farm, from the clutches of Rupert Melrose.

"Lady, you have to get down from there. I have a schedule to meet and I can't be lollygagging around here while you hold a meetin'." The stage coach driver spit on the ground and looked up at her. "Get down from there now before you fall and hurt yourself."

"I will get down as soon as I have an answer to my question." She looked around again. "Well? If there is no one here, does anyone have a brother, or son who is looking for a wife?"

Lord, she sounded like a dimwit. And at the moment that was exactly how she felt. But if she didn't get some man to marry her, and sign her agreement that he would help her keep her farm, then go on about his business, she would lose everything she owned. And since she ran out on Rupert earlier this morning, it was only a matter of time before he figured out what she'd done and come after her.

"Please?"

A rotund man who hadn't seen a razor in days, and

probably not a bathtub either, shifted a wad of tobacco from one side of his mouth to the other and leered at her. "I'll marry ya, little lady. I could use me a wife."

She gulped and tried her best to smile. "Thank you very much." Looking around, feeling a bit desperate, she shouted, "Is there anyone else?"

Her attention was caught by a man striding down the boardwalk, his glare and the sheriff badge glinting in the sun not a welcoming sight. She gave him her best smile as he approached the stage coach. "Are you applying, sheriff?"

"Get off there, now. You're creating a disturbance and keeping the stagecoach from leaving." He waved his hand, gesturing her to come down.

Calliope looked at the ground. Goodness, it was a long way down. Her back had been to the dusty street when she'd hoisted herself up and climbed onto the roof, settling in alongside the bags strapped there. "I'm afraid it's a long drop, sheriff."

The lawman fisted his hands on his hips. "You got up there, didn't you?"

A second man joined the sheriff, the grin on his face and humor in his eyes easing some of her tension. "Miss, jump and I'll catch you."

"Not until someone agrees to marry me." His eyes mesmerized her, made her insides clench.

He studied her for a few moments, then in a soft voice, said, "I'll marry you."

The sheriff turned to him. "Are you crazy, McCoy? The woman could be a criminal or loony, or both?"

The second man looked up at her. "Are you a criminal, or loony?" He still had the glint of mirth in his eyes. This man at least looked like he had a relationship with water and a razor. In fact, he was quite handsome. Black wavy hair that fell across his broad forehead. Piercing blue eyes never left her face, and didn't wander down her body like the first man's had.

"No. Just desperate."

He gave her a curt nod. "My offer stands, Miss. I'll marry you."

"Now wait a minute," the sheriff said, "you can't just up and marry this woman. You have no idea what she's all about."

"Unless you have a wanted poster with her picture on it back there at the jail, sheriff, you have no say in what this woman does. Or what I do." He looked up at her and reached out both arms. "Jump, and I'll catch you."

Why did she feel as though he meant a lot more than simply removing herself from the top of the stagecoach? "Are you sure, mister? You wouldn't be tricking me just to get me off so the stage can leave? I really do need someone to marry me."

"No. I'm downright serious. If you need a husband bad enough to climb onto the roof of the stagecoach and ask strangers to marry you, then I'm willing."

Why the devil was she hesitating? This is what she wanted, what she planned for when she ran out on Rupert this morning. This man was handsome, clean, kind, and the sheriff seemed to know him by name, so he must be an upstanding citizen. Why the uncertainty? She sighed and took a deep swallow. "All right." She shimmied to the edge of the roof and pushed off, landing with a thud into two strong, muscular arms.

"How do you do, Miss? My name is Stephen McCoy." Now that she was closer, she noticed the slight dimple in his left cheek and tiny scar near his full lips. He grinned at her as if this was all a joke. Not to her.

"Please let me down, sir."

"If I'm to be your husband shortly, I think I have the right to hold you in my arms."

His words slid over her like warm honey, causing a slight quickening of her breath. "Not yet, sir. Please release me."

With another teasing grin he set her on her feet.

Either the height of her stagecoach perch, or his disarming smile caused her to stumble a bit, slightly dizzy. He grabbed her arm, his brows furrowed. "Are you all right?"

"Yes, I'm fine." She smoothed out her skirts. "Is there a place we can talk? I have a few things I need to go over with you before we, ah, . . ."

"Marry?"

She nodded. "Yes."

"Just a minute, McCoy. As your friend, and peacemaker in Bartlett Creek, I insist on checking this woman out before I allow you to hitch up with her."

"Really, sheriff, do you think I would ride into town and make a public announcement if I was wanted by the law?" Now that she had a closer look at the other men who had gathered at her request for a husband, she didn't want to lose Mr. McCoy.

The sheriff pushed back his hat and scratched his head. "I don't know what to think, ma'am. All I know is this stagecoach has to be on its way, and I have to keep the peace. Do you have any luggage the driver needs to take off before he leaves?"

"Nah, she don't have nothin'. She got on the stage right outside of Sterling with nothin' but that bunch of flowers."

Mr. McCoy regarded her. "If you've been on that stage with nothing but flowers since this morning, I'm thinking you could use a meal right about now. Why don't we go on over to Bella's Café and have some dinner? Then you can tell me all about what it is you need to go over with me."

His suggestion was exactly what she needed. She was, in fact, pretty hungry right about now. Too nervous to eat her breakfast, she hadn't had a bit of food since supper the night before. Before she could even answer, he'd taken her by the elbow and moved her away from the stagecoach that was pulling out of the town.

"Go on. Y'all can go on about your business now.

The show's over. Miss—" Mr. McCoy looked in her direction with raised brows.

"—Bender," she supplied.

"Me and Miss Bender have things to discuss."

The sheriff shook his head. "I think you're plum crazy, McCoy, but seeing as how you're both adults, I'll leave you be." He pointed his finger at Calliope. "But I will be checking my wanted posters."

She allowed Mr. McCoy to escort her across the street and down a few stores to a small café. Now that she was half way through her plan, all she could think about was eating. Her stomach gave a very unladylike growl.

The café was small, but bustling with diners. Mr. McCoy grabbed a table near the wall, which gave them a bit of privacy. He held out her chair and then sat across from her. He leaned back in his chair and crossed his arms over his chest. "So why does a beautiful woman like you feel the need to ask strangers in an unknown town to marry her?"

Just then the waitress approached. "'Evenin', Stephen." She cast a curious glance at Calliope. "What can I get for you two?"

"I'll have the meatloaf." He looked at Calliope. "The meatloaf is very good, but so is everything else. In fact, the chicken and dumplings is the absolute best I've ever had." He grinned at the waitress. "Don't you dare tell Rosie I said that."

Rosie? Lord sakes. Did she just sit down to dinner with a man who accepted her proposal only to find out he was already married?

Want to read the rest of the story? You can purchase *Stephen's Bride* at most online retailers. Visit my <u>website</u> for more information or follow this link: <u>http://bit.ly/2fQjrw3</u>

ABOUT THE AUTHOR

Callie Hutton, the *USA Today* bestselling author of *The Elusive Wife*, writes both Western Historical and Regency romance, with "historic elements and sensory details" (*The Romance Reviews*). She also pens an occasional contemporary or two. Callie lives in Oklahoma with several rescue dogs and her top cheerleader husband of many years. Her family also includes her daughter, son, daughter-in-law and twin grandsons affectionately known as "The Twinadoes."

Callie loves to hear from readers. Contact her directly at calliehutton11@gmail.com or find her online at www.calliehutton.com. Sign up for her newsletter to receive information on new releases, appearances, contests and exclusive subscriber content. Visit her on Facebook, Twitter and Goodreads.

Callie Hutton has written more than 25 books. For a complete listing, go to www.calliehutton.com/books

Praise for books by Callie Hutton

A Wife by Christmas

"A *Wife by Christmas* is the reason why we read romance...the perfect story for any season." --The Romance Reviews Top Pick

The Elusive Wife

"I loved this book and you will too. Jason is a hottie & Oliva is the kind of woman we'd all want as a friend. Read it!" --Cocktails and Books

"In my experience I've had a few hits but more misses with historical romance so I was really pleasantly surprised to be hooked from the start by obviously good writing." -- Book Chick City

"The historic elements and sensory details of each scene make the story come to life, and certainly helps immerse the reader in the world that Olivia and Jason share." --The Romance Reviews

"You will not want to miss *The Elusive Wife*." --My Book Addiction

"...it was a well written plot and the characters were likeable." --Night Owl Reviews

A Run for Love

"An exciting, heart-warming Western love story!" --*NY Times* bestselling author Georgina Gentry

"I loved this book!!! I read the BEST historical romance last night...It's called *A Run For Love*.: --*NY Times* bestselling author Sharon Sala

"This is my first Callie Hutton story, but it certainly won't be my last." --The Romance Reviews

A Prescription for Love

"There was love, romance, angst, some darkness, laughter, hope and despair." --RomCon

"I laughed out loud at some of the dialogue and situations. I think you will enjoy this story by Callie Hutton." --Night Owl Reviews

An Angel in the Mail

"…a warm fuzzy sensuous read. I didn't put it down until I was done." --Sizzling Hot Reviews

Visit www.calliehutton.com for more information.

Made in the USA
Middletown, DE
27 July 2022